Working
New Beginnings Book 5

ROBIN MERRILL

D1521757

New Creation Publishing

Madison, Maine

Scripture quotation from World English Bible.

This novel is a work of fiction. Names, characters, businesses, organizations, places, events, and incidents are either the products of the author's imagination or used in a fictitious manner. Any resemblance to actual persons, living or dead, or actual events is purely coincidental.

We know that all things work together for good for those who love God, for those who are called according to his purpose. –Romans 8:28

Chapter 1

Esther

Esther's eyes scanned the sanctuary. She started to take a head count but felt a little like King David taking his census and stopped. Their small, upper-room prayer meeting had swelled so much in recent weeks that they'd had to move it downstairs. Esther had been a smidgen sad about that, but a gentle voice in her head had reminded her that change was a good thing. A church could not grow and resist change at the same time. And an abundance of prayer warriors was a good thing—especially when Derek was in the mood for howling like a wolf while everyone else was praying.

Pastor Adam called them all to order. Another thing she'd had to adjust to. She, along with her six friends—the founding mothers, her granddaughter called them—had been the ones to initiate and facilitate these weekly prayer meetings, and then suddenly Adam had taken over. Of course they were paying him for exactly such tasks, but still—it felt weird.

Today he seemed in a particular hurry. "Sorry to rush your fellowship." He leaned forward and rested his elbows on his knees. "I see that Derek isn't here yet, so I thought it might be a good time to discuss his situation."

All chatter stopped. No one looked at Pastor, as if they were all afraid to make eye contact with him. Esther forced herself to do just that.

"It is January," he started. "Last night it was well below zero. Do any of you know where Derek slept last night?"

No one responded.

"I don't either. I've asked him things like that in the past, but he is always reluctant to share details."

"He's a private man," Roderick Puddy said, sounding defensive of Derek.

"He is," Adam agreed. "But that doesn't mean he doesn't need our help."

"So what do you suggest?" Vicky asked, her face pinched.

Adam leaned back in his chair and sighed. "I don't have any suggestions. That's why I'm asking all of you."

"Isn't there a homeless shelter in Belfast?" Walter asked.

Esther cast him a sharp look. She didn't want to ship Derek back to Belfast. They'd never see him again.

Adam nodded. "There is, but they've kicked him out before. I'm not sure he's welcome back."

Walter's eyes widened. "Why'd they kick him out?"

Adam shook his head. "I'm not sure."

"Something about his dating life," Rachel said, and a snicker traveled around the circle.

"We've offered to let him sleep in our barn," Roderick said, "but he didn't want—"

"Your barn?" Barbara cried, horrified.

"Where have *you* offered to let him sleep?" Vicky shot at her.

Barbara's mouth snapped shut.

"Yes, our barn," Roderick said without looking at Barbara. "We don't have room for so much as a cot in our house, and I'm not sure I trust him alone with my children."

"Why not?" Walter asked.

Roderick shrugged. "I don't really have a reason, but I'm not sure where he's at mental health wise."

"He did pull a knife on Fiona," Rachel said thoughtfully.

"He did?" Adam cried. "I didn't know that!"

Rachel waved a hand at him. "It was a hundred years ago."

Esther snickered. It had only been a few months ago, but they'd been so busy that it did feel like a century had passed.

"What if we rented him a place?" Walter asked.

Esther's heart warmed at the suggestion. Walter was so smart and so generous. She had the urge to reach over and take his hand, but she didn't. This was prayer meeting.

Cathy shook her head. "That wouldn't work."

"Why not?" Vicky snapped. "Because you don't want to spend the money?"

Cathy closed her eyes in exasperation.

"Tightwad," Vicky mumbled under her breath.

"It's not that at all," Cathy said. "No landlord in Carver Harbor is going to want to rent to a homeless man. We'd have to pay first and last and a deposit and sign a lease committing us to a year of paying rent we might not be able to afford in a few months, and I don't even trust Derek to be here in a few months. We all know he disappears for days on end."

"He might not disappear if he had a place to lay his head," Vicky said.

"Fine," Cathy snapped. "*You* call around to the Carver Harbor landlords and see who is willing to open a homeless shelter at their property." Her gaze traveled around the room. "Or maybe one of you has a room you'd like to rent?"

Predictably, no one volunteered.

"What about that church that came down to help us with Levi?" Walter asked.

"From Mattawooptock?" Vicky cried. "That's two hours away!"

Walter shrugged. "Who knows? He might thrive there."

A judgmental rumble traveled through the room. How *dare* Walter suggest such a thing?

Adam held up a hand to stall it. "That's not a terrible idea. It might be the best thing for him, but I don't want him to feel like we're sending him away, like we want to get rid of him." He chewed on his bottom lip. "Why don't I bring up that church and make sure he knows about it. Then, if he acts interested, we can go from there? Until then, any other ideas?"

"What if we let him sleep here?" Esther asked.

It was Walter's turn to look shocked. "In the church?"

Esther didn't like his expression. It hadn't been a stupid suggestion. "That's what they do in Mattawooptock. What's the difference?"

"I think that's a great idea," Adam said. "I've thought of it myself. And I think such a thing may be in our future. But we're not set up for that yet." He held his hands out to his sides. "This place is huge. And old. With terrible insulation. We can't afford to heat it all day, every day. Maybe, with some updates and renovations, we would be able to, but those too would take funds we don't have."

Esther was impressed. Adam had thought this through.

"And this is a small town," he continued, "much smaller than Mattawooptock and more isolated. We don't have a homeless population here, and opening a shelter would probably attract homeless people to move here, which means we'd need to be prepared to do some political maneuvering." He looked around the room. "I'm not sure we have anyone with that skill set. Yet."

Esther wasn't so sure. She thought Walter could be pretty diplomatic when he wanted to be.

"It would also be a legal nightmare," Walter said. "I can't imagine the insurance we'd need to make sure we can't be successfully sued."

Of course. Leave it to the lawyer to think of that.

"Good point. And we'd need to have round-the-clock staff, either paid or volunteer. So anyway ... all right!" he declared, abruptly shifting his tone. "What is the next prayer request?"

Esther looked up to see that Derek had just walked through the front door.

Walter shifted uncomfortably in his chair.

"Don't worry," Esther said. "I don't think he heard us."

"I know he didn't."

Esther eyed Walter for a moment. Then what had him so fidgety?

Chapter 2

Cathy

Founding mother Cathy forced a smile as people flowed into the church for Sunday service. She had no reason to be so tired, but lately she'd been feeling quite rundown. Silently praying for some energy, she traveled around the room complimenting little girls' dresses and shaking adults' hands.

A man she'd never seen before walked through the front door. Something about him made her take notice. He was alone, but he stood tall and confident just inside the door, a leather-bound Bible at his side. Pastor must have noticed him too because he made a beeline to greet him.

"Who's that?" Jason DeGrave asked from right beside her.

She jumped and turned to look at him, happy to see his girlfriend, Chevon, by his side. "I have no idea who that is." She smiled at Chevon. "How are you feeling, honey?"

Chevon looked at the floor. "Fine."

"Don't you know everyone in town?" Jason asked.

She sighed. "That might have been the case once upon a time, but people come and go, and my memory isn't what it used to be." This was true, of course, but it was a moot point. She had a feeling she would remember that man if she'd seen him before.

Fiona started to play the pipe organ, and Cathy squeezed Chevon's hand as she stepped away. "You let me know if you need anything."

Chevon nodded meekly. She looked about as tired as Cathy felt.

Cathy found her way to her usual spot in her usual pew and then stared at the pulpit, waiting for Adam to welcome everyone, which he soon did. Then after a few brief announcements, Fiona began to play again, and Rachel stepped up front to lead the singing.

Cathy stifled a yawn as they went into their second hymn. She needed a nap, and she hoped Adam's sermon would be more lively than usual. Otherwise, her snooze was going to come at an inopportune time. She thought it would take Adam a while to forgive her if she snored during his sermon.

His message started off with a promising theme, but he was delivering it with his typical drabness. He was preaching from James, talking about how faith isn't much good if it doesn't translate into good works. She'd heard this sermon at least a dozen times before. She thought she'd even delivered this sermon before and probably done a better job of it. She fought off more yawns. But then Adam said something that made her sit up straight.

It wasn't his words so much as the look of uncertainty on his face when he said them. "I am issuing you all a physical, hands-on, boots-on-the-ground challenge." He gripped the pulpit with both hands, not saying anything else.

She raised an eyebrow. Did he want them to guess?

"Next Saturday, at eleven o'clock, I'm asking you all to meet me here. And we're going to leave the building in teams ... or maybe just one team. I guess that depends on how many people show up." He laughed awkwardly, and no one joined him. He cleared his throat. "Anyway, we're going to go door-to-door—"

Several people gasped in horror. Cathy realized after the fact that she'd been one of them. He wanted them to be annoying?

"No!" he said quickly. "Not like that! We're not going to preach at people and thump them with the Bible." He swallowed hard. "We're not even going to share the Gospel unless the Lord really gives you an opportunity to do that. Our goal is not to *proselytize*." He mispronounced the word, and Cathy ran a hand over her mouth to hide her involuntary smirk. "We're going to *serve*." He pronounced this word perfectly, and she began to catch on to what he was thinking.

And she *loved* it.

"We're going to knock on someone's door, introduce ourselves, and then ask what we can do for them. Do they need a meal? Do they need a ride somewhere? Do they need their snow shoveled?"

"People aren't even going to open their doors," Fiona mumbled from a nearby pew.

Surprisingly, Adam heard her.

"You're right, Fiona," he said. "A lot of them won't open their doors. And a lot of them will open their doors only to slam them in our faces. And some of them will say nasty things. But some of them will need our help, and then we will get to help them." He waited for more protests.

None were voiced, but Cathy could feel the objections heavy in the air. Her heart raced with excitement, but she knew not everyone was having the same response to this idea. She sneaked a look at her friends. Esther looked baffled. Esther never liked surprises. Vicky looked intrigued. Cathy didn't want to turn around and look at her back row friend, because she knew Barbara would be disgusted. She did turn to look over her left shoulder at Rachel, who caught her eye, grinned, and winked at her. She smiled back, unable to wink with her left eye. Then she scanned the room for Vera and found her fast asleep. Dawn sat beside her, staring at Walter Rainwater as if she hadn't heard a word Pastor had said. Cathy rolled her eyes. How anyone had the energy to have crushes at her age, she didn't know.

"We won't be able to get to every door in town, so I plan to do this for the next four Saturdays. And you don't have to do them all. You can show up once, twice, four times, or not at all. No one *has* to participate," Adam continued. "If you can't or choose not to show up on Saturdays, you are still very much welcome here on Sundays. But I hope I'll see you here on Saturday." He nodded. "I have a good feeling about this."

Cathy smiled. So did she. A very good feeling.

Chapter 3

Esther

"Get off the phone, Zoe," Esther said to her granddaughter, trying not to sound impatient. "We've got to go."

Zoe gave her an exasperated look. "I can walk and talk at the same time." She headed toward the door. "Please, come," she said into the phone. "It won't be so bad." She listened for a moment and then giggled as she stepped out into the hallway. "Thank you. Okay. Bye." She hung up the phone, beaming.

They stepped into the elevator. "Love sure does look good on you."

Zoe rolled her eyes. "No one said anything about love."

"Mm-hm." Esther wasn't buying that for a second. She knew love when she saw it. "So Levi's coming?" She pressed the ground floor button.

Zoe nodded.

"What was his hesitation?"

"Said he doesn't like people."

Esther snickered. "I could see why he might not want to participate in this little adventure, then." She wasn't sure she wanted to participate in this adventure. She wanted to help people, sure, but going door-to-door? What could she offer people? She should probably be asking *them* for help.

"I told him he wouldn't have to talk to anyone. I figured we could all hang back and let your *boy*friend do all the talking." She emphasized *boy*, and Esther gave her a dirty look. Zoe knew how much Esther hated calling Walter a boyfriend. He was a grown man, a *retired* grown man for crying out loud.

They stepped out into the cold, and Zoe zipped her coat up. "Doesn't look like many people are gonna show up." The church steps were empty, and there were only a few cars parked out front.

"I'm not surprised." Normally they cut across the lawn to get to church, but the snow was too deep, so they went to the street.

"I feel bad for Pastor," Zoe said. "He was so into this, and I'm not sure it's going to work."

"Well, we won't know if we don't try." Esther was pretty sure it wasn't going to work, though.

They started up the short driveway, and Derek fell into step beside them. "Good morning, ladies."

They both greeted him and then thanked him as he got the door for them.

"I'm taking Emma and Tonya!" Vicky declared as soon as they'd stepped inside. She had grown quite possessive of her two housemates.

About two dozen people swarmed around—more than Esther had expected. People must have carpooled.

"I want to go with them too!" Mary Sue Puddy declared. She started toward Emma, but her mother put an arm down over her shoulder and pulled her back.

"Not this time," Lauren said.

"Why not?" Mary Sue pouted.

"We're going to go as a family." It seemed Lauren wasn't so sure about this adventure either. She looked up at her husband. "We're going to stick together."

"That's right," Roderick agreed.

Pastor Adam finished splitting people into teams, most of which had already formed organically. He made sure each team had a vehicle and a cell phone. Then he gave each team a map of the town with a small highlighted section. Esther was impressed. Adam had done the prep work for this. She resolved then to make this work as best she could. For Adam. She admired his pluck.

Walter took Esther's hand and led her to the door, and Zoe followed. They met Levi coming in.

"Were you going to leave without me?" He sounded hopeful.

"Never." Zoe giggled.

Levi sighed. "Okay. Who's our first victim?"

Walter looked down at his map. "Looks like we're starting on Maple Street."

Levi nodded. "Good. I don't think I know anyone there."

Zoe giggled again.

Walter looked over at her. "Hey! This is our first double date!"

Zoe rolled her eyes, but she leaned into Levi as if she really were on a date.

They piled into Walter's Lincoln and weaved their way across town to Maple. Then Walter parked in front of the first house. He looked out Esther's window and up at the house and then looked at Esther again. "Well? Here goes nothing, I guess." He opened his door, and Esther, grateful for his bravery, followed suit.

She didn't know what she was so nervous about, but this was at least a mile outside her comfort zone. She let Walter lead, staying close behind him. Zoe and Levi hung back a few more feet.

Walter knocked on the door.

Nothing happened.

Walter knocked again.

The door cracked open, and a woman in a frayed pink bathrobe peeked out. "Yes?"

"Good morning," Walter said in what Esther assumed was his courtroom voice. "We're from New Beginnings Church, and we were—"

She slammed the door.

They all stood still, unsure how to proceed.

"Well, that went well," Levi said and turned to go back to the car.

"Hang on," Walter said. "No need to get in the car yet." He looked at the next house. "It makes more sense to walk."

"Maybe don't mention we're from the church this time," Zoe said.

"What?" Walter sounded annoyed. He didn't like unsolicited advice from a teenager, apparently. "That's what Pastor told us to do."

Zoe edged closer. "I know, but people hear the word church, and they panic."

Levi laughed, and Esther looked at him expectantly. He shrugged. "It's true."

"Fair enough. Let's try it." Walter walked boldly up to the next door. Esther got the feeling his efficiency stemmed more from wanting to get it all over with than wanting to serve God. She silently prayed this one would go better as he rapped his knuckles on the door.

This time, someone answered on the first knock. A younger man opened the door wide and looked them up and down.

"Good morning," Walter said. "My name is Walter, and my friends and I were wondering if there's anything we can do for you."

One side of the man's mouth curled up in a smirk. "What?"

Walter seemed to realize how crazy his pitch had sounded. "Right. As in, is there a way we can help you today? Anything you need?" He'd barely finished his sentence before the man shut the door in his face.

Levi laughed. "Two for two."

Walter looked at Esther. "I'm not sure this is going to work." He sounded embarrassed.

"I can talk at the next one," she said, even though she definitely did not want to do that.

"You think you can do better?"

"No, no," she hurried to soothe his ego. "I just want to give you a break."

He looked at the next house. "I don't need a break."

But at the next house, when the woman opened the door, Esther recognized her. "Brenda!" she cried with what might have been too much excitement. "How are you? I haven't seen you in ages!"

"Fine." Brenda looked back to Walter, who'd been cut off by Esther's joy. "What do you want?"

"We don't want anything from you," Walter tried. "We're going door-to-door and offering to help others."

"With what?"

"With whatever you need."

She sneered. "Oh yeah? Right now I need a new liver. You got one of those?"

Walter appeared speechless.

"No thanks," Brenda said and slammed the door.

The dispirited team turned to trudge down the walk.

"We're getting better," Levi said. "At least that one didn't swear at us."

"What?" Walter cried. "Who swore at us?"

Esther hadn't heard it either.

"Uh ... nobody. I was just kidding."

Chapter 4

Lauren

Lauren knew it was foolish, but she'd been so nervous about this whole ordeal that she'd hardly slept the night before. And now she was paying the price. She didn't have the energy or the patience for this, and she was being short with her children and her husband. Thank goodness no one else had joined their little team.

The first person they'd encountered had literally slammed the door in their faces. Judith was so shocked at the diss that she was now crying, leaving Lauren fiercely mad at the door slammer and also doubting her mothering ability—she shouldn't be taking a little kid door-to-door. What had she been thinking?

At the next house she offered to stay in the van with Judith, but Roderick had looked annoyed. "You're the one who wanted to do this."

This was most certainly not true. They'd never even discussed not doing it. Their pastor had announced it, and they had just done it—sans discussion.

"Fine," she snapped. "Mary Sue, stay in the car with Judith." She expected Mary Sue to complain, but she didn't. She was probably still too busy sulking over not being able to go with Emma's team. Lauren couldn't blame her. Being on the Puddy family team wasn't much fun.

To prove that she could do all this without her husband or his support, she marched up the walk and pounded on the door.

After a hesitation a woman answered. "Can I help you?"

"Good morning. My name is Lauren, and this is my family."

The woman looked over Lauren's shoulder at her laggard teammates.

"We are from New Beginnings Church, and we're going around town seeing if anyone needs any help with anything."

"Who is it?" a man's voice called from inside the house, and the woman jumped.

"Nobody. Just some church people," she called back.

Lauren studied her. "Are you okay?" she asked softly.

The woman nodded quickly and smiled widely. "Of course." She shifted her weight and then stepped back, looking down. "Um, we don't need any help, but thank you."

She started to shut the door, but Lauren stuck her foot in the way. The woman looked up in surprise as Roderick scolded, "Lauren!"

Lauren leaned closer. "We're in the old church on Providence Ave. If you need anything at any time, you come on by, okay?" She could hear the man approaching and stepped back. The woman looked her in the eye, held her gaze for a moment, and then nodded. She stepped back quickly just as he came into view, and then she shut the door.

"What was *that*?" Roderick asked through closed teeth.

"Not here." Lauren started back to the van.

He waited until he'd started the engine before repeating his question.

"She wasn't okay," Lauren said.

"What are you talking about?"

Lauren looked over her shoulder. "I don't want to discuss it with little ears around, but that woman needs our help."

He gave her an exasperated look and then looked in the rearview mirror at his children. "Does anyone need to go to the bathroom?"

"Yes!" a chorus rang out.

"We just went before we left the church," Lauren said.

"I know." He pulled the minivan into the road and headed back toward church.

Lauren didn't know what he was thinking but didn't have the mental space to care. She was too busy thinking about that woman. She mentally kicked herself. Why hadn't she asked her for her name? "What was that address?"

"I don't know. Something Pine Street. What does it matter?"

She stared out the window. "I was going to look it up online, try to find out the woman's name."

"Again, why does it matter?" He stopped in front of the church. "Mary Sue, take everyone in for a bathroom break. I need to talk to your mother."

Obediently, Mary Sue herded her siblings out of the vehicle and up the shoveled walkway.

"Lauren, what is wrong with you?" Roderick asked. He didn't give her a chance to answer. "I think we should call it quits. Try again next week when you've had some sleep."

She glared at him. "Well, that was patronizing."

His expression softened. "I'm not trying to be patronizing. I'm sorry. But this isn't like you, honey. You were almost aggressive with that woman. And what are you talking about, acting like she's in grave danger?"

For the first time, Lauren doubted herself. *Was* this just her active imagination at work? She avoided his eyes. "I think that woman is being abused."

He barked out a humorless, single-syllable laugh. "What?"

She didn't answer him. She wasn't sure how to.

"Why do you think that?"

She thought about how to explain it to him. "I just *felt* it. In the way she held herself. In the way she spoke, the way she jumped when he spoke—"

"He startled her." Again with the patronizing.

"It was more than that. And why would any woman be wearing that much makeup on a Saturday morning in Carver Harbor?"

He sank back into his seat and looked out the windshield. "*Oh, that's* what this is about."

"That's what *what* is about?" She wasn't following his thought process, but she *really* didn't appreciate his tone.

"You're judging a woman for wearing too much makeup, and you're—"

"What?" she cried. "I'm not judging anyone! What are you talking about?"

"Some people like to wear makeup, honey."

She wanted to strangle him. Yes, she knew that, of course. Just because she couldn't apply eyeliner without stabbing herself in the eyeball didn't mean she thought other women suffered the same disability. "I know that, Roderick." Her kids started drifting back out of the church, and she was glad. This conversation needed to be over.

"So let's not make assumptions—"

"I don't want to talk about this anymore," she said tersely as Peter slid the minivan door open. "That was quick!" She tried to sound bright and energetic like usual.

"Yeah, I didn't really have to go. I just wanted a doughnut." He started to slam his door shut, but the others were right behind him.

"Hey!" Victor cried. "Chop my head off, why don't ya?" Victor also held a doughnut.

"Did *any* of you go to the bathroom?"

"Yes," Judith and Carolyn said in unison.

"Three, four, five, okay, everyone's in!" Mary Sue said, and for the billionth time, Lauren silently thanked God for her eldest child.

The Puddy parents stayed silent all the way back to their assigned neighborhood. They didn't speak when they climbed out of the car and walked toward the next house. Lauren hung back and let Roderick do the talking.

The older gentleman who answered the door was civil enough, but no, he didn't need any help. Lauren was starting to think Pastor Adam's plan was a gargantuan waste of time, but then she saw the woodpile. Several cord of wood thrown into a messy pile covered in snow. She could see that someone had been drawing wood from the bottom of one side of the pile, but the pile was some distance from the house, and there wasn't even a properly shoveled path. She stepped closer. "Is that your only firewood?" As she asked, she looked up at the chimney to see if they had a fire going. If not, maybe the wood was their backup fuel. But she saw the telltale wood smoke curling lazily from the chimney.

"Yes, ma'am. Takes us about three cord to get through the winter."

Lauren considered her words. She didn't want to offend him, and she didn't want to further irritate her husband. "Do you have somewhere else to stack it? Somewhere under cover?"

He nodded, looking sad. "Years past, I've gotten it into the basement, where the furnace is, but I didn't get to it this year."

"We'll do it!" Lauren chirped.

The man stood up straighter as he raised his eyebrows. "Beg your pardon?"

"If it's all right with you, we'll put your wood into your basement, and we'll stack it neatly."

He looked at the woodpile and then back to her. "But it's all buried in snow. Lots of it is frozen together by now."

"That's okay." She didn't think she'd ever felt more determined. "We'll do the best we can."

He stared at them all for several seconds. "All right then. The name's Roger. I'll go around and unlock the cellar door." He shut the door, and Lauren looked at her husband, feeling triumphant.

He didn't look triumphant. "The kids are going to need gloves and snow pants."

"Go ahead and take Mary Sue home to get them. Victor and I can get started." She waited for Victor to complain, but he didn't. What a good boy.

Roderick shook his head. "Okeedoke. Come on, kids, let's go get some long johns on."

Chapter 5

Cathy

Cathy and Barbara gingerly headed up the icy path to their first house's front door.

Rachel grunted from behind them and then stepped in the snow to get around them and speed toward the door. "Slowpokes," she muttered.

Cathy watched her go, the wind making the feathers in the top of her hat dance. "I'm not bashful, Rachel. It's icy. You'd do well to watch your—"

Rachel cried out as one of her long legs shot out in front of her.

Instinctively Cathy reached out both arms to catch her friend, but there was no use. Rachel was too far away. And it turned out that a diving save wouldn't be necessary. Miracle of miracles, Rachel hadn't lost her footing. She had done a terrible version of a senior split, though.

"Ooooow," she cried as she pulled her feet back together and stood tall again.

Cathy was there in a second and grabbed her elbow. "Are you all right?"

"Go ahead." Rachel looked down at her legs as if to confirm they were still there. "Say I told you so."

"I would never," Cathy said, glancing at the front of the house. She fervently hoped no one was watching them.

"I told you so," Barbara quipped and then led the way to the door. "Let's get on with it. I'm cold." She went up the steps and knocked on the door.

No one answered.

Cathy looked up at Rachel. "Are you sure you're all right? You probably pulled a muscle."

Rachel straightened her hat. "I think I'm okay. I do my daily stretches at least once a month."

Cathy snickered. "Good for you." She let go of her arms and turned her attention to Barbara. "Well?"

"Well, what? They're not answering." She knocked again.

"There probably isn't anyone home," Cathy said. She looked at the unevenly shoveled path. "It might be safer to walk back through the snow."

"You can give me a piggyback ride," Rachel said and then cackled at her own joke.

The image made Cathy smile. If her slight frame were capable of giving anyone a piggyback ride, which it wasn't, it certainly wouldn't be Rachel the beanstalk.

Barbara knocked again.

Cathy wished she hadn't. "That's enough. Let's go. Either they're not home, or they don't want to talk to us."

Barbara looked put out, but she did turn away from the door and start down the steps.

"I'm going back through the snow," Cathy said and stepped into it. Rachel followed her.

"Nonsense. I can keep my feet under me."

For a second, Cathy wished she'd fall. But then she repented.

Barbara beat them back to the car, but not by much.

Cathy climbed behind the wheel, started the car, turned the heat up, and then hesitated.

"What is it?" Rachel asked.

"I think we should leave a note."

"What?"

Cathy shrugged. "If they're not home, we should leave a note." She leaned over and opened her glove box.

"Only you would be organized enough to have stationery and a pen in your glove box," Rachel said. "Mine is full of straws, cough drops, and hatpins."

"Sounds dangerous," Cathy said, but she was thinking about what to write more than she was thinking about Rachel's hatpins. She leaned forward and put the pad on the dashboard to give herself a better table and wrote, "Some folks from New Beginnings Church stopped by to see if your family needs anything. If we can be of service, call ..." She hesitated, wondering what number to write. Hers? Pastor's? She didn't know his offhand. She knew the church's number, but there might not be anyone there to answer the phone. *Put your money where your mouth is*, an annoying voice in her head instructed, and she wrote her own phone number on the paper. Then she ripped it off the pad, neatly folded it, looked at the house, and took a deep breath. "I'll be right back."

"Are you sure this is worth it?" Rachel said. "That path is treacherous."

Cathy had no idea whether it was worth it, so she didn't answer. She got out of the car and tromped back through the snow, her feet usually finding the footprints they'd already made. When these people got home, they were going to wonder what fruitcakes went stomping around in their snow.

She climbed the steps and started to stick the small piece of paper between the door and its frame but then jumped as the door was ripped open to reveal a red-eyed woman with a messy bun on the top of her head.

"Good morn—" Cathy started, flustered. Not sure it was still morning, she shifted to, "Hello! My name is Cathy—"

"We don't want any." She wobbled and grabbed the wall for support. The smell of alcohol wafted out toward Cathy.

Cathy tried to imbue her smile with love. "I'm not trying to sell you any—"

"We don't want any," the woman said again. She put a hand to her stomach.

A teenager came rushing to the door and wrapped an arm around the woman's waist. "I'm so sorry," she said quickly. "My mom's not feeling well." She spun the woman around and gently pushed her back into the shadows. Then she closed the door most of the way, only leaving enough space to peek out. "Can I help you?"

Cathy hesitated, but then the words found her. "We are from New Beginnings Church. We're going around town looking for ways we can be of help to people."

The girl narrowed her eyes. "You're asking everybody."

Cathy nodded quickly. That's why she'd phrased it the way she had, so the girl wouldn't feel singled out. "Absolutely. If you know of anyone in town who might need our help, we take recommendations."

The girl shook her head. "I don't. I don't know anyone. And we don't need any help. Thanks, though." She shut the door quickly, leaving Cathy staring at it, still clutching her note in her hand. She started to walk away but then thought she might as well leave her phone number and turned back to stick the note in the crack, half expecting someone to rip the door open again.

They didn't, though, and she made her way back to the car.

"Well?" Rachel said.

"They said they didn't need any help."

"You sound like you don't believe them."

"I don't."

"Well." Rachel sighed. "I'm sorry to say that I need some help. My groin is killing me. I think I need to go home, rub some arnica on it, and lie down."

"I could use a break too," Barbara said. "My gall bladder is killing me."

Rachel looked disgusted. "Why is your gall bladder bothering you now?"

"I might have dipped into the doughnuts before we left."

"I'll get you old broads home." Cathy put the car in drive. She gave the house a long look before driving away.

Chapter 6

Chevon

Chevon was beyond annoyed that the pastor had inserted himself into their team. It seemed he didn't trust three teenagers to go door-to-door and offer their help. What did he think they were going to do, toilet paper people's houses?

He wouldn't even let Jason drive, so Hype was up front in the pastor's car, happily chatting away as if they were best friends, leaving Jason and her jammed in the back.

She didn't feel good. She thought she might throw up again soon. So she wanted to stay in the car for the first house, but Jason insisted.

"Please? I know it feels weird, but this stuff can actually be fun once you get going."

"I'm not saying it's not." What did he think, that she was opposed to helping people? "But I've told you a hundred times that I don't feel good."

He grabbed her hand. "Right, but fresh air will help, and the moving around will distract you."

Neither of these things were true, but she was tired of arguing, so she got out of the car.

Pastor was already knocking on the door. *Wow, thanks for waiting.* A middle-aged balding man opened the door. He looked familiar, but Chevon couldn't place him.

"Good morning! We're from New Beginnings Church, and we were wondering if there's anything we could do to help you."

The man gave an incredulous smile as he took a second to study each of their faces. Chevon imagined he wasn't exactly finding the love of Jesus in hers. "You're kidding," the man finally said.

"No, sir. Is there anything we can do for you?"

The man let go of the door to fold his arms across the front of his white tank top. How warm did it have to be in his house for him to be wearing a tank top? A billion times warmer than it was outside. She pulled her coat tighter around her and grew even more resentful that she was out doing this.

"Now that you mention it, I need some money."

Pastor didn't seem surprised by this. He chuckled. "Well, we don't have any money, but whatever you were going to use that money for, we might be able to help with that?"

The man managed to scowl with his eyes while his smile stayed in place. The result made him look like the Grinch. "What's that mean?"

Good question. What *did* that mean?

"For example, if you needed groceries, we might be able to help get you some."

The scowl traveled from his eyes to his lips, and the smile was gone. "You're going to do that without money?"

Pastor nodded. "Yes, sir."

The man hesitated. "Fine, then. I need groceries." For some reason he looked right at Chevon when he said. "I like red meat the best. No vegetables." Then he shut the door.

She shivered, and she didn't know if it was from the cold or his creep factor. Either way, she was ready to get back into the car, and she headed that way.

She could hear the three men following her, but no one said anything until they got into the car.

"Well, that was a trip," Hype said.

"Yep. Let's go see if we can find the man some red meat."

"Seriously?" Hype said. "His beer gut suggested he's not exactly starving to death."

Pastor turned on his blinker. "The man said he needed groceries. We're going to give him groceries. Then maybe when he has a real need, he'll ask us for help."

Pastor parked in front of the church. "You guys can stay here. I'll run in and get him a bag of food."

Chevon exhaled in relief. She'd been certain Jason would want her to get out of the car again. "Jason? I *really* don't feel good. Do you think he would take me home before the next house?"

Jason took her hand again. "I'm sure he would, but please don't give up on this. I think it will be really good for you."

She rolled her eyes. Jason had been trying to talk her into Jesus ever since they'd started dating, and the more he pushed, the less interested she became. She yanked her hand away.

Pastor came down the church steps with two bags loaded with groceries. Hype opened his door to take them off his hands, and then they were headed back to the man in the tank top.

Pastor stopped the car and looked at Hype. "Would you like to do the honors?"

"What honors?"

"Would you like to deliver his food?"

Apparently, Hype wasn't sure. He looked at the house for a long time before saying, "Sure. Why not?"

Chevon watched him go up with the walk with a bag in each hand. Then he set them in front of the door. Chevon thought he was going to leave them there without knocking, and she thought this was hilarious. She couldn't wait to make fun of him for it. But then he knocked, shoved his hands in his pockets, and waited.

The man opened the door and looked down at the food with shock on his face. Then he and Hype exchanged words that she couldn't hear. But the smug smile Hype wore all the way back to the car annoyed the snot out of her.

Hype slammed his door shut behind him. "Thanks for letting me do that. That was cool."

"He was pretty surprised, huh?" Pastor asked.

"More like shocked. Then I told him that there was red meat in the bag, and he actually seemed touched, like emotionally." He looked at Pastor. "There *was* red meat in the bag, right? I didn't just lie to the guy?"

Pastor laughed. "No, there was steak in there."

"Oh good." Hype laughed uncomfortably. "Because that would've stunk if I'd lied to him. I would've had to go buy the guy a steak. And I don't have any money."

Pastor pulled over in front of the next house. "I've been meaning to ask. Why do they call you Hype?"

Chevon suppressed a groan. She'd only heard this story a thousand times.

Hype laughed. "I'm pretty good at sports, and when I was coming into high school, everyone was all excited, making a big deal of how good I was going to be and how much I was going to help the teams. So some of the upperclassmen started calling me Hype, as in I was all hype."

"Ah, I see. And were you?"

"Was I what?"

"Were you all hype?"

"I don't know."

"Mostly," Jason said from the back. Then he got out of the car without even looking at her.

Chapter 7

Chevon

The woman who answered the door at the second house leaned on a cane and wore a pink bandanna on her head. Chevon's stomach rolled at the sight of her. Suddenly, Chevon's nausea didn't seem that big of a deal. She looked at the pastor, worried he wasn't going to handle this well.

He greeted the woman warmly and introduced himself and then them. Chevon tried to smile but felt like a fraud. What was she doing out here, a pregnant teen with these Christians? Who was she trying to fool?

The woman put her hand to her chest. "I'm Natalie. Lovely to meet you."

Lovely? What was lovely about any of this?

Pastor repeated his pitch about wanting to help.

Natalie let out a high-pitched peal. It was weak yet somehow managed to sound joyful. "The good Lord's met all my needs, but I wouldn't mind your prayer." She touched the bandanna on her head. "I'm afraid I'm sick, and treatment's not going so well."

"We would be honored to pray for you." For the first time, the pastor looked unsure. "I don't want to impose, but I don't want to stand here letting all your heat out either." He smiled. "As we pray," he added.

"Oh! Of course!" She stepped back. "Come right in!"

Chevon was the last to step into the warm, neat kitchen. It smelled like rosemary. This made Chevon's mouth water, which was shocking. She hadn't been hungry for days.

"Welcome to my humble abode."

"Thank you for inviting us in. I don't know if you know this, and speak up if we start to freak you out." He laughed awkwardly. "But the Bible tells us to lay a hand on the sick when we pray for them."

She waved a hand. "Oh I know all about it. Lay away."

Pastor gave Jason a nod and at the same time, they each lay a hand on the woman's frail shoulders. They left Hype and her completely out of it, and she was grateful. She sneaked a look at Hype, and he looked as uncomfortable as she felt.

"Father in heaven," the pastor began and immediately got choked up. Chevon looked at him, surprised. Didn't he do this sort of thing all the time? "I thank you for your daughter, Natalie. I can see your grace in her, and I thank you for that testimony. Thank you for bringing us here today to be blessed by her faith, and please show us a way to bless her in return." He paused and took a long breath. "Father, we boldly ask you for a supernatural work here. We ask you for a miraculous healing. We know you sent your son so that we might have life abundant, and we ask for that abundant life here. We ask you, in Jesus' name, to come against fear, to come against pain, to come against illness. We boldly ask you to cure Natalie so that you may be glorified through her healing. And in agreement to this, we say ..."

"Amen," the pastor, Jason, and Natalie said in unison.

"Amen," Chevon mumbled shortly afterward, feeling foolish, embarrassed, and hopelessly out of place.

Natalie wiped at the tears streaming down her taut cheeks. She smiled up at the pastor. "Thank you so much. I appreciate that."

He squeezed her shoulder and then let go of her to reach for his wallet. Chevon thought he was going to give her money, but he pulled out a business card. "Can you think of anything else we can do for you?" He looked around the room. "Do you need any supplies? Any food?"

She shook her head. "Oh no. I'm all set, thank you."

He handed her the card. "If you need anything, you call anytime. It's been an honor to meet you, Natalie, and I'd love to see you again. We have service every Sunday at ten-thirty, and of course you're welcome, but even if you can't make that, we're still here for you."

She nodded, and there was a weird knowing in her eyes, like she knew so much about life, which made Chevon feel like she knew so little.

The pastor smiled at Chevon, making her even more uncomfortable. "Okay, kids, let's go."

Being called a kid annoyed her beyond belief, but Natalie looked at her just then, distracting her from this irritation. "When are you due?" Natalie whispered.

Chevon startled and looked down at her belly to see if she was showing yet, though she knew she wasn't—especially through a winter coat.

"Oh, you're not showing yet, dear. I just have an eye for these things. That's all."

"June," Chevon managed, though her voice sounded thick, unlike her.

Natalie winked. "Congratulations. It's going to be wonderful."

Chevon held her gaze for a moment but then realized Jason was holding the door for her. "It was nice to meet you," she said lamely.

"And you as well," Natalie said.

Chevon turned away from her and allowed Jason to lead her outside and to the car.

She slammed the car door, suddenly overwhelmed with so much emotion she couldn't process it.

"What's wrong?" Jason asked.

"What's wrong?" she cried. "What did we just accomplish exactly?"

Pastor answered the question she'd meant for Jason, which further enraged her as he wasn't even supposed to be there. "We prayed for healing, and God does heal people. And we let her know that we are here for her if she ever needs us."

"She's not going to need us," Chevon said before she could stop herself, "because she's going to be dead."

"Chevon!" Jason said, appalled that she would dare speak the obvious.

She rolled her eyes and leaned against the car door, wanting to get as far away from him as possible. This whole project was so stupid. Bothering sick people, making them cry, giving them false hope, making her meet and really like a woman who was going to die any minute. Stupid, stupid, stupid.

Chapter 8

Chevon

No one spoke as the pastor parked his car in front of their third house. But then Jason looked at her and said, "Maybe you should sit this one out."

Tears sprang to her eyes. She would rather have died than cry right then, but she couldn't stop it. She rubbed away her tears so hard that she hurt herself.

"Hey," Jason said softly as if talking to a child. "It's okay."

Her body started shaking with fury. "I know it's okay," she said through gritted teeth. "I never said anything about anything not being okay. I just don't appreciate being treated like a child."

He reared back and glanced toward Hype's seat, but Hype had already gotten out of the car, as had the pastor. "I'm not treating you like a child. You said you don't feel good, and you were kind of mean at the last house—"

"I *don't* feel good!" She fought to keep her volume down. "I *never* feel good anymore. Ever since you planted a human inside of me."

His eyes widened. "So this is *my* fault?"

Pastor rapped on the window. "We'll take this one without you guys."

"No!" she screeched. She got out of the car and slammed the door behind her as hard as she could, hoping to break it. Punish this grown man for pushing himself into their plans. They could've handled this without him and then maybe Jason wouldn't be being such a jerk.

Wiping her eyes again and sniffing, she stomped toward the door. Then without waiting for the men, pounded on it.

A plump older woman answered the door promptly. "Well, hello there." Her smile quickly fell into a pitying look. "Oh dear, are you okay?"

On no. What had she done? What was she doing? She stepped back quickly to let the pastor take over.

He readily gave his spiel, and the woman was quite receptive. She seemed delighted this bunch of weirdos had knocked on her door.

"This is so nice of you young people, but the only thing I can think of that I need help with is my cat."

"Oh?" Adam said.

"Yes, he seems to have run off." As she spoke, her joy at seeing them faded, and grief took its place. "I miss him so much." She looked around. "I've asked the neighbors, but no one has seen him."

"What does he look like?" Adam asked.

"He's an orange tabby. He'll come right up to you and rub against your legs. He's so friendly." Her eyes were wet now.

"Sorry that this has happened," the pastor said, "and we will certainly keep an eye out for him. In the meantime, if you think of anything else you need, you let us know."

She nodded.

"Or maybe we'll see you Sunday?"

She nodded again.

The pastor started to back away.

"Wait," Chevon said before she knew she was going to speak.

Everyone looked at her.

They were all going to leave? They finally had something they could help with, and they weren't going to do it? This woman wasn't like the gross red meat guy or the dying woman. This woman had a solvable problem. Chevon tried to smile at her. "What's the cat's name?"

"Hissy Fit," the woman said, her voice laden with love.

Hype snickered.

Chevon wanted to take three steps and kick him in the shins, but she forced herself to focus on the woman. "Do you have a picture of him?"

"Of course. I have many. Hang on." She gently shut the door.

"Shut up, Hype," Chevon muttered.

"It's a good idea," the pastor said. "The photo, I mean, not the shutting up."

The woman returned quickly with a framed photo. She held it out toward Chevon but kept it inches out of her reach.

"Oh, he's beautiful," Chevon said. "I'm so sorry he's missing. Have you put up flyers around town?"

"Oh no. I hadn't thought of that."

"We can do it for you." Chevon held out her hand. "If you wouldn't mind me making copies of the photo."

She hesitated. "Will I get it back?"

"Of course. And soon. I just need to make some copies."

The woman handed it over. "Thank you, dear."

Chevon smiled, and it was the first sincere smile she'd smiled in days. "And can I have your phone number? To put on the flyers? Or do you want me to use mine?"

"Oh no," she said quickly. "You can use mine. Hang on." She closed the door again.

"Not a word, Hype."

"I wasn't going to say anything. I just didn't know you were such a cat lover."

He would know that if he'd paid any attention to who she was, but he didn't. Just like his best friend, Jason. Who she was going to marry.

The door opened again, and the woman handed Chevon a scrap of paper. "My name is Fanny if you want to put that on the sign too."

"Great. Thanks." She shoved the scrap of paper into her pocket. Her fingers were growing numb.

"No, dear. Thank *you*."

"You're welcome. We'll find him." She didn't know how she knew this, but she did. She turned and headed back to the car, her companions close behind.

Chapter 9

Chevon

The church was abuzz with excitement. It seemed the others had had far more fun with this than Chevon had.

The pastor called everyone to order. "Let's report back. I'm thinking some of our teams might have been asked for help that other teams might be better equipped to give." He scowled and looked around the room. "Where are the Puddys?"

No one answered. Zoe shrugged and pulled her phone out of her coat pocket. Then she laughed. "I was thinking I could text Mary Sue, but she doesn't have a phone."

"Do any of the Puddys have a phone?" the pastor asked.

"Lauren does," Vicky said. She looked at Esther. "Don't you have Lauren's number?"

She did, but she didn't have her phone on her. They started to squabble. Vicky was mad that Esther didn't have her phone handy, and Esther was quick to point out that neither did Vicky.

The pastor held up both hands. "Never mind. I'm sure they'll show up any second." He sat down. "Okay, I'll report first. At our first house, the gentleman asked for money, so we brought him some groceries. At our second house—"

"Why didn't we give him money?" a woman asked. Then she looked embarrassed. "I mean, if he was in need, couldn't we give him some money?" It took Chevon a minute to place her. Then she realized it was Levi's mom. When had she shown up? She hadn't been there in the beginning.

"That's a good question, Nora," the pastor said. "I asked him to be more specific about his needs, and he made a joke about wanting steak. So I don't think he was in dire straits. But he knows who and where we are now, so if he ever is in real need, I hope he'll ask." He looked around the room. "And who knows? Maybe this goes so well that we make another round and check on him again in a month."

Chevon groaned quietly.

"Anyway, at our second house, we met Natalie. She is battling cancer, and we prayed over her. I'd like to pray again for her right now, if you guys would help me with that."

Everyone nodded somberly and bowed their heads. Chevon did not bow her head. She looked around the room in wonder that everyone else had. What an obedient bunch. What a bunch of lemmings. Good thing the pastor wasn't handing out Kool-Aid.

The prayer took a really long time, and her mind drifted to her to-do list. She was anxious to get home and start making the flyers.

Finally, they all said, "Amen," and the pastor said, "Okay, Walter, would you like to report next?"

What? What about their third house? What about Fanny?

"Not much to report," Zoe's grandmother's boyfriend said. "Everyone slammed their doors in our—"

"Wait," Chevon interrupted.

Everyone stared at her.

Not again. She gave the pastor a sassy look. "We also went to a third house, where we met Fanny, whose cat is missing." She expected him to take over and finish her report, but he didn't, so she turned to the rest of the group. "She gave me a picture, and we're going to put up flyers around town so if anyone sees him, they can call her."

"We?" Hype muttered.

Jason elbowed him. "Yes. *We*."

"That's good, Chevon. Thank you."

Again, she didn't appreciate the pastor's patronizing tone. Why was everyone treating her like she was a little kid? "Maybe we should pray for the cat too," she said and immediately wished she hadn't. She had no idea how this praying thing worked. Was it stupid to pray for a cat? Was it disrespectful to God? There had to be rules about such things.

"I think that's a great idea," Esther said. "Good thinking, Chevon. What's the kitty's name?"

Chevon hesitated. She was embarrassed to say the name aloud. The silliness of it made the whole situation seem silly, and she didn't think it was. But everyone stared at her expectantly.

"Hissy Fit," she mumbled.

"What's that dear?" Esther said.

Again Chevon hesitated.

"Hissy Fit," Hype repeated. "The kitty cat's name is Hissy Fit."

Chevon glared at him.

"Oh, what a great name!" Esther declared. "All right, everyone, back at it." She bowed her head, and everyone followed suit.

This time so did Chevon.

"Father in heaven," Esther prayed softly. "Thank you for being a God who cares about problems of all sizes. And we know that if this woman shared her missing cat with us, then it's not a small problem to her. So we ask you now to reach into that situation. Comfort that woman, encourage her, help her not to fret and worry and imagine horrible things. And Father, we ask you to find that cat. Whether through us or someone else, we ask you to bring that cat home. In Jesus' name we pray. Amen."

Chevon didn't pick up her head. She didn't want anyone to see that she was crying again. She didn't even know why she was crying. So she kept her head bowed and let the tears drip onto her jeans.

Chapter 10

Lauren

The line of cars parked along the curb made it clear that everyone else had already returned to the church, which made sense, as they were supposed to be back by one o'clock. The firewood had taken longer than Lauren had thought it would. The red rawness on both her hands testified to the duration of the project. Still, she was glad they'd done it. She hoped Roger and his wife would think of God every time they drew from the neat stack of firewood in their warm, dry basement.

She herded her children up the steps and into the building. It seemed they'd just finished praying.

"Ah! Welcome home!" Pastor said. "We were a little worried about you."

Lauren frowned. "Not too worried. My phone didn't ring."

"Honey," her husband said softly as if he was afraid that she was about to lose it and tell the pastor off.

"You're right," Pastor said, as unoffended as he should have been by her innocent comment. "We weren't that worried. Also, I don't have your phone number. Could I get that? Yours too, Roderick, if you don't mind."

"Sure," her husband said.

Lauren looked around for empty chairs. There weren't enough. She found one and pulled Judith into her lap. Let the others fend for themselves. She took a deep breath and tried to calm down.

"How did your team do?" Pastor asked, looking at her.

She opened her mouth to answer, but before she could utter a word, Roderick said, "We didn't have much luck until the third house, where an elderly couple needed their wood stacked, which we did. It's all neatly thawing out in their basement now."

Adam looked impressed. "Awesome!" He clapped his hands. "That's what I'm talking about! Thank you for doing that." His eyes drifted from Roderick. "Tonya, would you like to report next?"

Lauren cleared her throat. "Honey, you forgot about the second house."

He gave her a tired look. "I didn't think there was much to say. They didn't want our help."

"I'm concerned about the second house," she said more loudly. "The woman looked—"

"Lauren," Roderick said firmly. He'd been annoyed since she'd first expressed her concern, but this was the first time he'd sounded angry. It shushed her, made her doubt herself. She trusted his wisdom, his judgment. Maybe he knew something she didn't know. Maybe she shouldn't go making accusations in front of this many people. But now she'd made the proclamation, she didn't know what to say next. She looked at Pastor sheepishly. "I don't know. The woman just didn't seem okay. Can we just pray for her?"

"Of course," Adam said quickly. "Let's do that right now. What's her name?"

Lauren's cheeks grew warm. "I didn't get a chance to ask it," she said, her voice fading with each word. She was suddenly way too hot and wished she'd taken off her coat before she'd sat down and propped an almost-sleeping child on her lap.

"No problem." Adam seemed eager to help her save face, and she was grateful. "God will know who we mean. Would you like to do the honors?"

"Go ahead," Lauren said quickly. She bowed her head and then added, "Thank you."

"Father, we're back," Adam said and let out a long breath. "Seems we're going to need your help with lots of these people, and that makes sense. So we lift up this woman that Lauren met today, and we ask you to interfere with her life, Father. We ask you to wrap your arms around her and let her feel your love in a real way. Let her hear your voice and soften her heart so she will respond to your call. If this is someone you want us to minister to, please open that door, and if Lauren is meant to be that connection, then please tell her how to do it. Show her the way, Lord, and equip her to do what you want done. We pray your will be done in this woman's life and in all the lives of all the souls in Carver Harbor. In Jesus' name we pray. Amen."

Lauren lifted her eyes and met her husband's. He didn't look pleased.

Chapter 11

Chevon

Chevon watched the Puddy mother pray and then watched her pick up her head and look at her husband. Something was wrong. Chevon had no idea what it was and wasn't sure she cared, but there was something the Puddy mom wasn't saying. Chevon looked to Mary Sue for a clue, but her face betrayed nothing.

"Okay," the pastor said. "Tonya, I believe you're next."

Emma's mom took a deep breath. "The first house we went to has a broken chimney." She looked around the circle. "I was wondering if Barbara's son knew anything about chimneys, but I don't see her here."

"Yes," one of the older women said. The one with good hair. Chevon knew she should know her name, but it wasn't coming to her. "Her gallbladder was bothering her, so she went home."

A few people winced, and a bunch nodded as if this was a common occurrence.

"And Rachel slipped on the ice and hurt herself, so she went home too."

Several people gasped, and Esther acted particularly panicked. "Is she all right?"

The woman with good hair waved her off. "She'll be fine. Anyway, back to Kyle. I'm sure he knows how to fix a chimney, but I'm not sure we'll be able to get him to. He's booked up way in advance, and he's often reluctant to work for free. How broken is this chimney? Are these people without heat?"

Tonya shook her head. "No, they're making do with electric for now."

Good-hair-woman gasped. "That's going to cost a fortune!"

A man across the circle from Chevon said, "I'd be happy to hire someone to fix their chimney. Just give me their address."

Pastor's mouth dropped open. "Wow, Joe. Thank you. That is so generous."

Joe waved him off, but his expression was smug. "Don't mention it."

"Great!" Tonya looked thrilled. As she shared the encounter she'd had at their second house, Chevon studied the man across from her.

She remembered him from Sunday, how he had walked in alone with his nose in the air. How the pastor had practically tripped over himself to shake the man's hand. She didn't like the way he was sitting, leaned back in his metal folding chair as if that were comfortable, with his arms folded across his chest and his left ankle resting on his right knee. His foot dangled effortlessly. He looked like the most comfortable man in the world, but Chevon wondered how much effort he was putting into that effortlessly dangling foot.

"I'd be happy to give Max a job," Joe said.

Chevon looked at Tonya. She had missed who Max was.

"There's room for him at my company in Bucksport."

"But you don't have any idea what he's good at," Vicky said, her face pinched, her eyes narrowed, "or if he's good at anything."

Oh good. Chevon wasn't the only one suspicious of this guy.

"What's your name again?" Vicky asked. If she narrowed her eyes any further, they'd be shut.

The man smiled broadly. Too broadly. "Joe. Joe Weir."

"Joe has just joined us, and we're so glad to have him," the pastor said.

Chevon looked at the pastor. Then she looked at Mr. Joe Weir again. Certainly a pastor was a better judge of character than she was. Maybe the guy wasn't so bad. Maybe she was just being cranky because she was pregnant. Yeah, that was probably it. And yet, there was something about him. Something off.

Joe Weir caught her eye and smiled at her. Yes. Definitely something off.

"How did you do at the third house, Tonya?" the pastor asked.

"Pretty good. They were friendly, but the only need they had was their single daughter living in their basement. They asked us to find her a mate."

Joe uncrossed his arms to fling them out in front of himself, palms out. "Sorry! I can't fix that one!"

Everyone around the circle laughed as if that were the funniest thing they'd ever heard. Chevon looked at Jason with an expression that said, "What on earth?" but Jason didn't even see her. He was too busy gazing at Joe Weir and laughing right along with the rest of them.

Chevon bit her lip. She must be missing something. This guy was a real hit with the Jesus-peeps. Yet more evidence she didn't belong with the Jesus-peeps.

Chapter 12

Esther

E sther winced as she sank into the restaurant chair Walter had pulled out for her.

"Are you all right?" He sat across from her, his brows furrowed with a concern she had no doubt was genuine. He was so adorable.

"Yes, I'm fine. Only a little sore from all the traipsing around we did yesterday. I'm surprised I'm not sorer."

"What did you think of all that?"

The question surprised Esther a little. He wanted to know what *she* thought about it? "I don't know," she said carefully, wanting to sound intelligent, not wanting to disappoint. She tried to find words. "Ask a more specific question."

He chuckled and leaned back in his chair. "I'm not sure I have one. Maybe ... do you think it's a good idea?"

Think what was a good idea? Helping people? "What do you mean?"

"I mean going door-to-door, knocking on strangers' doors, interrupting their day ... I'm not so sure I'm on board."

"You certainly don't have to participate."

He tipped his head sideways and gazed at her, a small smile on his lips. "As if I'm going to let my lady, in her words, *traipse*, around town without me."

Her cheeks grew warm. She started to take her sweater off.

"It might be exactly what God wants." He shrugged. "I'm still learning about what God wants."

"We're all still learning." She stopped fidgeting and made herself look at him. He was so strikingly handsome. How did she ever end up in a relationship with such a youngster?

"Do we really need to go looking for problems to solve? So far with your little church, problems have come right to your door when they needed you."

He had a point.

"You mean *our* little church." She smiled. "I don't know. These questions are too hard. Ask Cathy."

He chuckled and reached across the table for her hand. "I don't want to ask *Cathy*. I'm not looking for a right or wrong answer. I want to know what *you* think."

"Oh. Well. I think it's a good idea. It probably won't always go smoothly. Obviously, because it didn't for us. But what if we find that one person who goes to heaven because they encountered Jesus through us?"

Walter's expression relaxed. "That's an excellent point. And it probably trumps all others."

She was thrilled to hear this and relieved that she probably wouldn't have to say more.

The server approached, greeted them, and asked what they wanted to drink. Walter was his usual charming self, and she walked away grinning.

"People probably wonder why you're at a romantic restaurant with your mother," Esther said before realizing she shouldn't say things like that.

He laughed. "No one is wondering any such thing. Our ages are not that different, and at our age, who cares?" His expression grew serious. "I wanted to ask you something else."

Oh no. More hard questions.

He took a deep breath and looked down at his hands, which he was wringing. What was this? "I ... uh ... I was wondering ... no pressure ..."

Was he nervous? He hadn't acted nervous around her in ages.

His hands let go of each other, and he drew them down his face. "Ah, I rehearsed this, and I'm still blowing it."

"Maybe you shouldn't have rehearsed it."

He chuckled, and his shoulders relaxed. "Thank you for making me laugh. All right, I want to throw something out there, only for discussion. There is no expectation and there is no pressure. I only want to get a feel for where you're at, and if you don't know where you're at, that's fine too."

Esther held her breath.

"I've been thinking about Derek."

Breath rushed out her. Oh, thank God, he only wanted to talk about Derek. She'd feared he'd wanted to talk about their relationship.

"I've been thinking that I live in a giant house by myself, and he sleeps outside." His words sped up as he delivered them. "So I was thinking how can I claim to be a Christian if I don't offer him a room?"

Esther gasped. Walter was a brand-new believer. She couldn't believe he would think of that. She certainly hadn't, and she'd been a believer forever.

"And I'm not like Roderick. I don't have any children to consider. It's just me rattling around alone in that house. But I have hesitated because you're my girlfriend, and I want you to be more than my girlfriend. Not right now, of course, we only started dating, but down the road, and maybe not so far down the road, Esther, I would hope you would consider being more than my girlfriend, so I don't want to offer him a room without first checking with you to make sure that's all right. But how do I check with you without making you uncomfortable and pushing you too fast?" He laughed loudly, humorlessly. "Do you see the pickle I'm in?"

She was speechless. There was so much to process, she didn't know where to start. She opened her mouth to respond, no words came out, and she snapped it shut again. But then she saw the discomfort on Walter's face and knew she had to say *something.* "I think it would be amazing of you to offer Derek a room."

He hesitated. "That's it?"

She wanted to say more but didn't have the words.

"What about everything else?"

"I'm not sure," she said slowly.

He looked away, nodding, and exhaled slowly. "All right. I guess that's fair."

She studied the tablecloth. It was a lovely shade of ivory. She wondered how they kept them so clean.

"And in the future, if we were to decide to take this relationship to the next level, how would you feel about you and Zoe living in a house with Derek?"

Whoa. *Zoe* living in a house with Derek? Zoe was sixteen. So she would likely be leaving Esther soon. That meant that Walter was thinking about taking this relationship to the next level *soon.* Her mouth opened and closed soundlessly again.

"I'm sorry. I know you wanted to take things slow. I'm just scared of extending this offer to Derek and then having to yank it away, or having you say no to moving in with me because Derek lives there. I know he's a little crazy."

"Moving in with you?" Esther realized after the fact that she'd said the words aloud.

"Well, no. I mean, yes, of course. I mean ..." He sighed and ran his hands down his face again, as if trying to wipe off the last few minutes and start again with a fresh face. "Of course I would hope that one day you would share a home with me. But that would only come after we were married. I know the rules. And I'm not asking you to marry me today or to move in with me today. I am happy to move at this pace we're currently enjoying and explore these things in the future. But Derek is cold *now*, so he's forcing me to think about these future things."

Esther didn't know what the future held. She hadn't even considered marrying Walter. They weren't there yet, and she didn't think she'd ever be there. Of course she was crazy about him, but she'd already been married. In so many ways, she still was married. Her husband was in heaven, but their marriage was still so much a part of her.

"I'm sorry. Maybe I shouldn't have asked."

"No," she said quickly, wanting to comfort him. "You should have. And yes, I definitely think that if you think God wants you to invite Derek to live with you, then you should absolutely do that. And if the time ever comes when ..." She couldn't bring herself to say the words. "When we consider the next step, I will have no problem with Derek no matter where he lives."

Breath rushed out of Walter. He leaned his elbows on the table. "Oh, thank you, Esther. That's what I needed to know." Then he laughed contemplatively. "But now I realize part of me hoped you'd forbid it." He leveled a gaze at her and bit his lower lip. "Because now I have to invite Derek to live with me."

Chapter 13

Chevon

"Come on, let's go," Chevon said.

Jason had already eaten two sandwiches and was now polishing off a large bag of chips one crumb at a time while he stared at the football game on television. "What's your hurry?" he said around the food in his mouth, not looking at her.

"Oh I don't know. It's wicked cold out, and the cat is lost out there somewhere."

Jason stood up licking his fingers. It was hard to think of this as a victory, though, because she was pretty sure the chips were gone.

"Okay. But this just proves how much I love you."

This proved no such thing. "Isn't this what you Christians are supposed to be doing with your time? Helping others?"

He leveled a gaze at her. "It's a *cat*."

"Yes, it's a *cat*. Are you saying God doesn't care about cats?"

Jason took a deep breath, looking exasperated. "Yes, I think I'm saying that God doesn't care about cats."

She didn't know much about God, but she didn't think this could be true. Maybe Jason wasn't as smart as he thought he was. "Well, even if he doesn't care about cats, he cares about the lonely old woman who lost hers."

Something seemed to click in Jason's head because he nodded. "Good point. Okay, let's go."

It was her turn to roll her eyes. Finally, she was getting him out of his house.

He looked at the clock on the wall. "Gotta get outta here anyway. My mother will be home soon."

Ah yes, it was always important to avoid Alexis DeGrave, who was intent on pretending her son hadn't impregnated his classmate. She also liked to pretend she hadn't had an affair with a pastor and ripped his family apart.

"Do you have the flyers?"

She wanted to smack him. Of course she had the flyers. "Yes, it doesn't take more than twenty-four hours to make flyers. I posted the picture all over the Internet and I've printed a hundred flyers. We just need to put them up."

His jaw dropped open. "A hundred flyers? Are you nuts?"

She glared at him.

"I thought we were putting up like five? There aren't even a hundred windows in this town. Are we driving up to Bucksport too?"

"We aren't limited to windows. I was thinking telephone poles."

He tipped his head back and closed his eyes. "How are you going to tape them to telephone poles?"

"There's a stapler in your car, right beside the flyers that I printed. Can we please go?"

He opened the door. "Your wish is my command." He actually managed to sound lighthearted, so he obviously had no idea how irritated she was.

She stomped outside and to the car, not giving him enough time to open her door for her even though she was growing to appreciate that gesture. As silly as it was, it made her feel special. Of course, she wasn't going to tell *him* that.

It turned out that she didn't need the stapler. The first telephone pole was covered in nails from other people's signs, signs taken down or blown away long ago. She wondered how many animals had been posted on this pole, animals that had never made it home. Tears threatened, and she shook them away. That wasn't going to be the case with this one. They were going to find Mr. Hissy Fit. She needed something good to happen. She stepped back and watched the flyer flutter in the breeze. She knew it wasn't secure and she knew that Jason was about to tell her that, so she rushed back to the car to grab her duct tape. She hurried back to the pole, pulled off a long length of it, and ripped it off the roll with her teeth. Then she wrapped it all the way around the pole, securing the top of the paper to the damp wood. She did the same at the bottom. Then she stepped back, satisfied with her work. She was feeling better already, and the cat wasn't even rescued yet. Cold now, she hurried back to the car.

"Did you invest in duct tape stock before you did that?" He laughed at his own joke.

She was too happy to be annoyed.

"That's not going to last through any rain."

"I know that," she snapped. "It's not going to have to last long. We're going to find him."

"I really don't want to do a hundred of these."

That was rich as he hadn't even gotten out of the car.

"What if we get some help?" he asked.

"I already texted Hype. He couldn't even be bothered to answer me."

"That sounds about right. What about Zoe?"

Chevon held back a sigh. It was hard not to be irritated with how close Jason and Zoe were. She knew their relationship wasn't like *that*, but it still irritated her. She hated that she was jealous and tried not to be. "Fine. Text Zoe."

"You do it. I'm driving."

She fished her phone out and invited Zoe to come hang signs.

Zoe answered immediately. "Can Levi come?"

As if she was going to say no to that. She'd never been close to Levi, but he'd rescued her from her coatless walk to school, and he was rapidly growing on her. She appreciated a person who absolutely did not care what other people thought about him. "Obviously."

"Cool. Where are you?"

Chevon told her to meet them at the Mobile station. Then she instructed Jason to go there. She went inside and asked for permission to hang a flyer in the window. The clerk regretfully told her that corporate would not allow them to do that. Annoyed, she came back outside and taped a flyer to the outside of the window. She knew somebody would take it down soon, but it was still satisfying. Sticking it to corporate and all that.

It was still too soon for Zoe and Levi to show up, so she walked to the nearest telephone pole, hung a flyer on a nail, and did her duct tape trick. She relished the sound of duct tape being pulled from the roll. What a cool noise that was. Made her feel like she was handy.

She walked to the next telephone pole. And then the next. She hit every pole within a reasonable walking distance and then returned to the car to find Jason playing on his phone. "You could help, you know."

Jason looked up. "I didn't know you were going to walk all over town. I thought you were only going into the store."

Chevon looked down the street for any sign of Levi or Zoe. "You know, we'd probably be done already if we didn't waste time sitting here waiting for them."

"Oh, will you please stop!"

She looked at him, surprised at his sharp tone.

"I get that you're pregnant and that's hard and all, but you're taking the crazy pregnant woman to the extreme. You're really not much fun to be around right now."

She bit her lip and looked away as her eyes grew hot with tears. "Sorry."

He sighed and reached over to take her hand. "No, I'm sorry. I'm sorry that you don't feel good, and I'm sorry that you're upset about this cat thing. But I really do wish you would just relax and try to enjoy life a little. Even when it's messed up."

That was easy for him to say. He wasn't pregnant.

She saw Levi's mom's car in her side mirror. "They're here." She wiped at her eyes with the back of her free hand.

Levi sauntered up to Jason's window, which Jason rolled down. Levi rested on the sill. "So do you want us to take half the stack of cat signs, or is this like a double date thing?"

Jason laughed. Then he looked at Chevon and held his hand out. Regretfully, she gave Levi half the stack. It's not that she wanted them to climb in the car with them, but she was a little sad to relinquish some of her project. She tipped her head back against the head rest and closed her eyes. "Thanks for the help, Levi. And thank Zoe for me too." She let out a long breath. Jason was right. None of her emotions made any sense. She *was* crazy.

Chapter 14

Lauren

Lauren lay awake in the dark, staring up at her ceiling. Her husband snored softly beside her. She should get up. She'd been trying to fall asleep for hours and hadn't. It was pointless to continue lying there.

But her body didn't move. She was too tired to accomplish anything. Besides, she comforted herself, doing chores would wake the children up. Their washing machine squealed like a banshee caught in a bear trap. And if she ran any water at all, weird, unexplainable bursts of air in the pipes shook the whole house. She could sweep, she told herself. Sweep in the dark. But then she decided she'd rather lie there and stew about the sad woman with the mean husband.

You don't know that, she chided herself. She didn't know the man was mean. It wasn't fair to accuse him, even silently in her own head.

But she *did* know that. Somehow, she knew it. She'd seen it in the woman's eyes.

Lauren squeezed her eyes shut. She'd lost count of how many times she'd prayed that night, but it obviously hadn't been enough. *Father*, she said silently in her head, *I pray again for the woman with no name. I pray you protect her, save her, deliver her.* Another voice in her head interrupted her prayer, accusing her, telling her she was crazy. *Father,* she concentrated harder, *if this is all my imagination, please give me your peace about the situation. If you flood me with reassurance that the woman is safe the way she is, then obviously I will lay off. I don't* need *her to be in danger. I just think that she is. But I don't know that. So please, if I'm wrong, please take away this worry. Take away my obsessing. Replace my anxious thoughts with your overpowering peace and let me fall asleep.* She paused, pleased with this plan. It was a good one. *In Jesus' name I pray.*

Keeping her eyes closed, she waited. She waited for the powerful peace to descend onto her. But it didn't come.

And she didn't fall asleep.

An hour later, she swung her legs out of bed and tiptoed across the room to the small desk where their laptop sat. She tried to be sneaky as she opened it and fired it up. It booted up slowly, reluctantly, and she glanced back at Roderick to make sure she hadn't disturbed him.

He hadn't moved.

The computer chimed that it was on, and Lauren directed it toward a website that showed her satellite images of Carver Harbor. She had to guess at the address, typing in 9 Pine Street and then 11 Pine Street until 15 Pine Street was the winner. There it was. The house. Now what?

She typed the address into a search engine, but nothing helpful came up. So she typed, "How to find out who lives at an address." A page full of advertisements loaded, each offering names, personal details, and background checks, making Lauren feel like a total creeper. She scrolled past the ads and clicked on the first non-sponsored website, which promised answers but then wouldn't deliver without a fee. She kept scrolling, but each of the websites was the same—until she found an article titled "Three Free Ways to Find Out Who Lives at an Address." Bingo. She clicked and waited.

Method number one was to knock on their door and ask. She rolled her eyes in the darkness. She could have thought of that one. Method number two was to go to the local library and check the voter registry. She'd never heard of such a thing, but the Carver Harbor library's winter hours were Tuesdays noon to five, or something like that. It certainly wasn't open at four o'clock in the morning on a Wednesday. Her eyes flitted down to option three: property tax commitment book.

She furrowed her brow. Tax maps, of course. But that would only work if they owned, not rented. Still, it was better than lying in bed looking at the ceiling, so she navigated to the Carver Harbor tax maps and then clicked on the commitment book PDF.

When that had downloaded, she searched it for 15 Pine Street and quickly found the home was owned by Trevor and Molly Lariken. She stared at the names. They didn't ring any bells. She'd never heard the name Lariken, so she didn't think they were local. But it was still possible. Was that even them, or were those the landlords' names? She searched her social media site for Molly's name, and a photo popped up. Yep, that was her.

"What are you doing?"

She jumped. Roderick was standing right behind her.

"I'm trying to figure out that woman's name."

Roderick sighed and bent to turn on the desk lamp. Then he sat on the foot of the bed. "Look at me."

She didn't.

"Please." There was a gentle kindness in his voice.

She turned in her chair.

"Is this about your mom?"

She narrowed her eyes. "Don't."

"I'm not trying to pick a fight, honey. But you're being unreasonable about this, so I'm trying to figure out why. And all I can think is that something about that woman reminds you of your mother."

"So what if it does?"

"So what ..." His frustration obvious, he stopped to keep from expressing it. "So that's not fair. To anyone. That woman didn't look scared to me. She wasn't bruised. She didn't ask for help. You are obsessing over an ordinary woman, and I think it's because of some buried trauma in your own head—"

She reached behind her and slammed the laptop shut. Then she got up, went to the bed, grabbed her pillow, and headed for the door.

"What are you doing?"

"Going to watch television."

Chapter 15

Chevon

Chevon still wasn't feeling well, but she wanted to get out of the house, so she agreed to a date night. Jason had promised her it would be romantic.

And all things considered, he was doing a pretty good job. He'd driven her to Fort Wagner, but the snow prevented them from getting close to the water. He'd seemed really disappointed by this realization, which she found endearing. She also found the sparkling cider endearing. The red solo cups and the bologna sandwiches, not so much.

"I'm sorry, Jason. It's not your fault." She zipped the sandwich baggie back up, wishing she hadn't forced herself to take it. "Most foods make me sick."

"I'm sorry." He sounded like he meant it. "I should've asked you what you wanted." He sighed. "But unfortunately, I was limited to what my mother had in the kitchen. And she's not exactly Martha Stewart."

She chuckled. "It's okay. Really. I've basically given up on all food." This wasn't true. Ritz crackers and pickles were still her friends. But she didn't want to eat crackers and pickles in Jason's car. She didn't want to smell like vinegar.

He zipped his sandwich into a bag, also unfinished. "I wanted to talk to you about something."

Oh, good. They hadn't had a real conversation in too long. "Okay. Shoot."

He took a deep breath. "I don't want you to feel like I'm pressuring you or anything ... because I'm not."

She tensed. She didn't know where this was going and already she felt pressured. "Okay," she said again, less enthusiastic this time.

"I guess I'm just wondering where you're at with Jesus."

She groaned. "Are you serious?"

"Of course I'm serious."

She didn't want to talk about this. "Hey, you want to discuss childbirth instead? How my body's about to be ripped open and how much that's going to hurt?"

He looked at her. "Huh?"

"Yeah, because I'd rather talk about that than talk about religion."

His eyes turned back to the windshield, and he looked so sad that she felt bad.

"Look, I'm sorry. I love you, Jason, but can't we just agree to disagree on this? We don't have to agree on every—"

"But why don't you?"

"Why don't I what?"

"Why don't you agree with me on this? You've heard what the Bible says. Do you not believe it's true?"

She leaned back against the headrest. Apparently they were going to discuss this whether she wanted to or not. "I don't know, Jason." Neither did she care, but she didn't think she should say that. She didn't want him to totally freak out. "I've just got a lot of other things"—more pressing things, she thought without saying—"on my mind."

He nodded, his jaw tense. "I understand that."

"Do you? So can you just calm down about the religion?"

He jerked, and she regretted her words.

"Not that you're not calm. You are. You've been pretty patient with me. But I'm going to church with you. I went to the stupid Saturday thing. Isn't that enough? What do you want from me?"

He took a long breath, and it sounded shaky, which alarmed her a little. Jason had seemed so strong lately. "It's not what I want from you. It's what I want from Jesus."

It was her turn to say, "Huh?"

He closed his eyes. "What I've come to expect from Jesus. Look, when my adulterous mother became the butt of every joke, I thought my life was over. I was so embarrassed I didn't think I could live through it. But there was Jesus. And he was a friend. No, more than a friend. I can't explain it, but he was there, and he brought me so much comfort. And then my parents announced their divorce, of course, and then again, I thought I wouldn't survive the shame, but he was there again. I talked to him, and often, in weird ways, he talked back. I was never alone, and I was never hopeless. I knew that whatever was coming was going to come and that I would survive it because of him."

Part of her wished he'd stop preaching at her. Part of her was riveted. This was the most he'd talked to her in weeks.

"And then you. When I found out you were pregnant, Chevon, I was so terrified. It felt worse than anything I'd been through. I thought the guilt would literally kill me. I felt guilty for messing up your life, guilty for cheating on Alita, guilty for causing a pregnancy, guilty for judging my mom and being so mad at her when I'd done something just as stupid." He paused. "Well, *almost* as stupid. Anyway, I didn't think I'd survive it, but there was Jesus." He looked at her. "And I know you're struggling right now. And I get it. I'm not saying you shouldn't be struggling. I try to imagine what you're going through, and I can't really. I'm sure it's awful. But I know how much he could help you." He swallowed hard. "But only if you let him."

This was the most enticing presentation of Jesus she'd ever heard. "That's some good preaching," she said, and it came out far more sarcastic than she'd meant it. She opened her mouth to try to get her foot out of it, but he didn't give her a chance.

"Fine. You're right. I can't make you choose the truth. But how can you ignore everything that's happened? How can you ignore Zoe getting sober?" She hadn't known Zoe was ever drunk. "How can you ignore us finding Levi in the middle of nowhere? That was all because of Jesus!"

She looked down at the pathetic sandwich she still held in her hands. "I'm not ignoring that stuff, Jason. I'm just ..." She searched for the right words. "Like I said, I just can't process it right now. You're asking me to trade in my whole world-view, the one I've spent my *life* forming, for yours, which doesn't even make sense to me. That's not an easy thing to do, especially not when I'm throwing up all the time and staggering around too tired to think."

He sighed. "You're right. I'm sorry." He turned to her abruptly and pulled one of her hands away from her sandwich.

His touch sent a warm jolt up her arm, and she smiled despite herself.

"I love you, Chevon. I love you more each day. Every time I look at you, you are more beautiful. And your lack of faith scares me."

She pulled her hand away. Lack of faith? Could he be more judgy? More condescending?

He grabbed her hand again. "The Bible says we're not supposed to be unequally yoked. I want to be yoked to you. I'm just scared what's going to happen if we don't get equally yoked."

Chevon had absolutely no idea what he was talking about. Yoked? As in egg yolks? But she was too tired to ask. "I think you should take me home now."

He hesitated, staring at her.

"I'm not mad or anything. I just don't feel good and want to go to bed. Please, just take me home."

Chapter 16

Chevon

Chevon was still annoyed about last night's yolk conversation when Jason showed up at her door. Oh yeah. It was Saturday. Time for another round of lunacy. She opened the door and tried to be polite as she invited him in. She didn't feel very welcoming and didn't think she was faking it well.

He stepped inside and looked around nervously. Then he looked her up and down. "Are you ready?"

She was still in her pajamas. "Jason, could I sit this one out? I really don't feel well." Despite her overwhelming exhaustion, she hadn't slept much the night before.

His face fell. "Really?"

"Yeah. Really. Hey, my parents aren't home. You want to hang out here? We could watch a movie or something?"

He looked confused. "I can't. I have to go do this."

"You don't *have* to do anything," she said, her anger rising. He would rather go pound on strangers' doors than spend time with his sick, pregnant girlfriend? She waved at the door. "Fine, go."

"Wait, why are you mad at me? What did I do?"

"You didn't do anything." She moved toward the door, trying to herd him in that direction.

He took one step and then stopped. "Is this about last night?"

"No, Jason. Not everything is about you," she said, even though this was very much about him.

"I didn't say that it was. Well, then, if you're not mad at me ..."

She didn't remember saying that.

"... then you should come. What about the cat lady? We'll go check on her."

"Fanny." Chevon folded her arms across her chest, suddenly remembering she wasn't wearing a bra. Shoot. She'd forgotten all about Fanny. And Hissy Fit. It had been almost a week since they'd hung their signs. He was right. She did want to go check on Fanny. Maybe Hissy Fit had come home. If so, she needed to know. She needed some good news. Reluctantly humbled, she looked up at him. "I need to get dressed. Will you wait for me?"

He looked relieved. "Of course. Take your time."

She gave him a small smile. His words tempted her to drag her getting ready out, but she was too curious about the status of Hissy Fit. She grinned going up the stairs. Esther had been right. That *was* a great cat name.

Ten minutes later, when Chevon stepped outside, she had second thoughts. With the wind chill, it had to be well below zero. She zipped up her coat, which was starting to feel a little too snug across her stomach. She couldn't be sure that was the baby, though. The gallons of ginger ale she'd been drinking probably weren't helping her avoid extra weight gain. She shivered.

"Come on, let's get the car warmed up." He hurried toward her door and opened it.

Jason's car was old and in no hurry to heat up. It made her wonder how they were going to manage the coming changes. He couldn't afford a car with heat. How were they going to raise a baby? When they pulled in front of the church, the car was still frigid, but she was warmed by the memory of the promises made by the ladies of the church.

That was how. That was how they were going to raise a baby.

She looked up and down the street. "Looks like we've lost some soldiers."

"Probably." He reached over and squeezed her knee, which felt amazing and made her smile. "Thanks for coming. This is so much more fun with you here."

She nodded and watched him climb out of the car. Then she realized she was just sitting there like a lump, and she climbed out too. He took her hand and led her up the shoveled path toward the large front door.

They were definitely late, but everyone was still sitting in the circle. Maybe others were in no hurry to venture out into the sub-zero temps.

"Could we just pray that someone opens the door for us today?" Esther asked and then tee-heed.

"Certainly," the pastor said. "Any other requests?"

"Not so much a request as a praise," Joe Weir said as Jason led her to a seat. "Just wanted to report back on some things from last week. The Mortellos' chimney has been fixed, and Max Barrack is now gainfully employed at my company."

There was a spattering of applause, and then those who hadn't clapped at first succumbed to peer pressure. Chevon didn't clap. Who was this guy praising, exactly? God or himself?

"That's awesome!" the pastor said. "Praise God!"

Good. They were praising God.

"And thank you for all you've done to make those miracles happen," the pastor added.

Okay, praising Joe Weir too.

The pastor's eyes found hers. "Any word on the missing cat?" He sounded sincere.

Not liking the feeling of all eyes on her, Chevon slowly shook her head. "We're going to check in with her today. The woman, I mean, not the cat. The cat's a boy." Her cheeks got hot, and she looked at the floor.

"That sounds great, Chevon. Good job. Cathy is going to go with you today, as her other teammates are still ..." Chevon lost track of his words because she was looking at the woman the pastor was pointing at. The one with good hair. Something about her rubbed Chevon the wrong way. She was nice enough, but Chevon found her a little ... she wasn't sure of the right word. Uppity? She was a little *too* put together.

She tried to remember which note Cathy had written for her baby shower. What had she promised? Chevon couldn't remember. She could go back and check, though. She still had the notes. She planned to keep them forever. She planned to give them to her baby when she grew up. She touched her belly, warmed by that thought.

Cathy caught her eye and gave her a kind smile that made Chevon feel guilty. She might be uppity, but that wasn't the worst thing in the world. And did this mean the pastor wouldn't be infiltrating their team today? If so, Cathy joining was a good thing.

The pastor prayed and then handed out maps and assignments. With less enthusiasm than the week before, the teams headed out into the cold. Jason stopped and looked at his car. Then he looked back at the steps.

"What?" Chevon asked.

"I'm wondering where Cathy and Hype are."

Chevon turned to stare at the steps with him. "This Cathy lady. What's her deal?"

"What do you mean?"

"I mean, is she nice? Is she cool?"

"Oh yeah. Definitely. She's very nice. And wicked smart."

Hype came out the door and down the steps with his hands in his pockets.

"Is Cathy coming?" Jason called to him.

"Who's Cathy?" he called back.

Chevon rolled her eyes and shivered. "I'm really cold. Maybe we should wait inside."

Jason looked at her. "You should get a better coat."

This comment enraged her. "Yeah, I totally should. Because my parents want to buy me a new coat, even though this one cost nearly a hundred dollars, so that I can go stand on a church lawn for no reason."

Jason stared at her like a deer in the headlights.

"Do you youngsters want me to drive?" Cathy had appeared on the lawn, wearing a coat that looked like a sleeping bag. "My car is very comfy." She studied Jason and Chevon. "Or I'm happy to ride with you if that's better."

"No thanks," Chevon said through gritted teeth. "Jason's car has no heat."

Chapter 17

Chevon

"My car has heat," Jason muttered as he buckled up. "Sorry."

"You embarrassed me."

How could such a small comment to an old church lady embarrass the great Jason DeGrave? Whatever. "I said I was sorry."

He leveled a gaze at her. "And yet I don't believe you."

Cathy pulled away from the curb.

"Where to?" Hype asked with an irritating eagerness.

"Well ..." Cathy glanced in all her mirrors as if she was looking for a tail. "Pastor gave us a map, but I thought we'd visit the cat lady first." Her eyes caught Chevon's in the rearview. "Do you remember the address?"

"Not exactly, but it was right by that dead artist's house."

Cathy chuckled.

"Wow, way to be specific," Hype said.

Chevon was so tired of being embarrassed. "I can't remember his name."

"I know just who you mean." Cathy turned on her blinker. "Let me know when you see the cat lady's house."

Chevon didn't have to, though, because Hype did the honors.

Cathy put the car in park. "Why don't you boys stay here. I'll leave the heat on."

"What?" Hype sounded offended. "Why?"

"I don't want to overwhelm the woman."

Suppressing a grin, Chevon climbed out of the car and waited for Cathy to catch up before heading for the door.

"I don't think we'd overwhelm her," Chevon said quietly. "There were four of us last time."

"That was just an excuse." Cathy raised her knuckles and rapped on the door. "I thought you needed a break."

Fanny ripped the door open, her smile so bright Chevon was sure that Hissy Fit had found his way home. "Well, good morning! I saw the young lady coming up the walk and I thought she was here about Hissy Fit, but then I saw you, Cathy! Come right in! I haven't seen you in ages! Can I get you some coffee?"

Cathy stepped inside, and a little dumbfounded, Chevon followed.

Fanny shut the door behind them. "Good morning, Fanny. It's lovely to see you." Cathy embraced the woman, gave her a good squeeze, and then stepped back. "Chevon, Fanny and I used to work together at the mill."

"Work *together*," Fanny said. "You make it sound like we were equals." She looked at Chevon. "Cathy was my *boss*. And she was quite the taskmaster!" She tee-heed and then waved them toward a cluttered kitchen table. "Come on in! Have a seat! Let me pour you some coffee."

Chevon didn't want coffee, but she was a little amused at the idea of the boys waiting in the car, wondering what they were doing in here.

"We can't stay long, Fanny. Let's get together for coffee later. You were right. We're here about Hissy Fit. Chevon and I are both members of New Beginnings Church ..."

This wasn't true. Chevon hadn't joined anything.

Fanny's face fell. "I'm sorry to say he's still missing."

Chevon's chest tightened. This was not the way this was supposed to go. "We hung signs all over town," she said quickly. "Has anyone called?"

Fanny gave her a long look. "Did you bring back my picture?"

Shoot. "No, sorry. I forgot. But I will."

Fanny narrowed her eyes in suspicion as if Chevon was attempting a cat-photo heist.

"I will," Chevon repeated.

"No, no one has called, I'm afraid."

This wasn't good. It was so cold outside. Maybe Hissy Fit wasn't going to be able to come home.

Fanny set a steaming cup of coffee on the table near where Cathy stood.

Cathy ignored it. "How long has he been missing?"

"Oh now let me see ..." Fanny stared at the ceiling. "I last saw him around Halloween ..."

Halloween? Was she serious? The cat had been missing for more than two months? A tangle of emotions overwhelmed Chevon. Embarrassment. She was an idiot. She hadn't thought to ask the woman how long the cat had been missing. Anger. The woman hadn't thought to tell her the cat had been gone for ten weeks? She'd made it sound like he'd just wandered off yesterday. Sadness. This cat was definitely dead. And back to embarrassment again. She was going to *beg* Cathy not to tell Jason and Hype. And then gratitude that Cathy had left them in the car. Her eyes welled up with tears.

"Oh, you're such a dear to care so much," Fanny said, sounding sincere. "Bless your sweet heart."

Cathy stepped closer. "I'm so sorry, Fanny." She reached for her arm. "That's a long time for a cat to be gone."

"I know," Fanny said matter-of-factly. "I had given up, but when the church people asked me what I needed help with, that's what came to mind. They gave me a bit of hope after nearly a year of not having any."

Wait. What?

"A year?" Cathy repeated calmly. "You said you saw him around Halloween?"

"Oh, yes, sorry." Fanny tee-heed again. "I meant *last* Halloween."

Her words sucked the air out of Chevon. The storm of emotions clobbered her from multiple directions, dizzying her. She reached out for something to steady herself, but there was nothing there. She tried to gasp for air, but her body didn't cooperate.

And then just as she was about to slide down into a useless puddle, a strong hand grasped her arm. Cathy was right beside her, holding her up. "I'm sorry, Fanny. We've got to get going, but can I stop by later for that coffee?"

Fanny stared at Chevon. "Are you all right, child? You're white as a ghost."

"She's okay," Cathy said before Chevon could think about an answer. "She's not been feeling well, so I'm going to get her out of here, but I'll see you soon."

"All right."

Cathy turned her and nudged her toward the door. Surprisingly, her feet cooperated and then even picked up speed.

"Don't forget Hissy Fit's picture!" Fanny called after them.

Then they were out the door and the piercing cold felt great. Chevon sucked in a lungful of it.

Still holding onto her arm, Cathy shut the door, led her a few steps down the walkway, and then turned to face her, grabbing her other arm. She looked into her eyes. "I know you're not up to snuff. Is it emotional or physical?"

Tears that Chevon didn't even know were threatening to do so spilled down her cheeks. "Both," she said weakly.

Cathy nodded, unsurprised. "Okay. The boys don't need to know about the cat. No one does. Ever." She raised an eyebrow. "Capiche?"

Something about her tone calmed the chaos in Chevon's brain. Or maybe it was the fresh air. She exhaled. "Capiche."

Chapter 18

Cathy

D riving toward what was supposed to be their first house, Cathy thought back to her own pregnancies. They hadn't been easy. She'd worked full-time, through the morning sickness that lasted all day, through the emotional roller coaster rides. And she hadn't been an unwed teenager.

Poor Chevon. Cathy glanced at her in the rearview. She was a little less pale now. Still pale, but not quite as ghostlike. The kid had almost passed out in Fanny's kitchen. Cathy silently thanked God that she hadn't.

She stopped in front of a Cape Cod with peeling red paint. There were four cars in the driveway. It would be difficult to pretend there was no one home. She turned to look at Chevon. "You want to sit this one out?"

Sheepishly, she nodded.

"Good idea. You give that baby a break. I'll leave the car running." She climbed out, expecting the boys to follow, which they did.

A woman answered the door, her lips pressed into a thin, pale line.

"Good morning!" Cathy tried to sound cheery. "We are from New Beginnings and we are going around town checking on people, seeing if they need anything."

Her eyes narrowed. "New Beginnings? What's that?"

"It's a church on Providence Ave."

"And you're just going around town banging on doors?"

She hadn't banged on anything. "That is correct. We're looking for ways to serve the community."

A young boy with something brown and sticky all over his face sidled up to the woman and wrapped a shirtless arm around her leg.

"Get back, Devon. It's cold out. Go get a shirt on."

The boy vanished, and the woman looked at Cathy. "My kids don't have boots yet."

Oh wow! Cathy hadn't been expecting that. "We can probably help with that! What sizes?"

"I don't know. Hang on." She shut the door in their faces.

Yes. This was more like what she'd expected.

She and the two teenage boys stood there awkwardly, silently, for a long time.

"Do you think she's coming back?" Hype asked.

"Not sure," Jason said. "And I'm not sure how long we stand here before we accept that we've been duped."

The woman opened the door and handed an envelope out to Cathy. "These are their sizes."

Cathy took the scrap paper and looked at it. "Oh wow, you have five kids?" She hoped this would lead to a new family attending their church. She loved the idea of five more kids running around.

"Yes, and no girlie colors please."

Cathy looked up, surprised.

"My girls don't like pink or purple." She started to shut the door. "Or yellow." She shut the door the rest of the way.

The deadbolt clicked into place.

Cathy let out a long sigh. "Come on, gentlemen, let's go see if we can find some boot funding."

Pastor wasn't at the church, but Joe Weir was.

"You didn't join a team today?"

"I offered to man the fort," he said with a broad smile.

"Oh." She returned his smile. "I just need something from the office." She headed toward the corner of the building and pulled open the top drawer of the filing cabinet. Inside it was a money pouch full of cash. The women had decided to keep it on hand in case there was a crisis during non-banking hours. She took out some twenties and then slid the door shut, turning toward the doorway—which was filled with Joe Weir. She jumped. "Sorry," she said a little breathless. "Didn't know you were standing there."

He frowned. "That's not a very secure place to store money."

"No. You're right. But there's not much in there." She started toward the door, but he didn't move. "We plan to get a safe. Just haven't gotten around to it yet."

He still didn't move.

"If you'll excuse me."

"Did someone in town ask you for money?"

Something inside her chest started grinding. Was he serious? Did he think she was *stealing*? He had no idea who she was! "Are you going to let me out of this room?"

His face relaxed, and he stepped back swiftly. "So sorry! Didn't mean to block your exit. That's a small room!" He was obviously trying to sound nonchalant, lighten the moment.

It didn't work.

"It's an office. Not a gym." She headed for the door.

"But what's the money for?"

She turned to face him. Then she paused, considering her words. "Sir, I don't know you, and I know you don't know me. But I'm a founding elder of this church, and I answer to God—not you." She waited a beat and then turned on her heel and walked outside.

"Are you okay?" Hype asked.

She followed his eyes to her hands on the wheel. They were shaking. "I'm fine, thank you. I think I just have low blood sugar."

"I have some crackers," Chevon said quickly. "Would you like some?"

"No, thank you, dear. Let's go to Reny's, get some boots, and then I'll treat us all to a snack."

"I can't keep much down other than crackers."

"That's okay. I'll buy you a ginger ale."

Chapter 19

Lauren

"You want me to drop this?" Lauren said.

Her husband stared straight out the windshield—silent.

"Then let me go back there and check on her. If everything's hunky-dory, I'll let it go." She knew it wouldn't all be hunky-dory. She'd prayed for peace about the situation. She was experiencing the polar opposite of peace.

Roderick sighed. "Fine. But I'm going with you. And this time when she tries to shut the door, let her."

Fair enough. "Thank you."

They were quiet for a minute. Even the kids in the back were.

"And whether this satisfies you or not, if they don't give you hard evidence you can take to the police, you're going to have to let this go. Otherwise they're going to feel harassed. And I don't think that's the testimony we want to give."

Lauren looked out her window. She hadn't been thinking about her testimony.

When they reached the house, Lauren beat her husband to Molly's door. She tried to make her knock sound polite.

Immediately the door opened to reveal a handsome, smiling man. His flannel shirt was tucked into his dark blue jeans. He wore a belt. His beard was neatly trimmed, and there was gel in his hair. Lauren found the combination of these details discombobulating.

"Can I help you?" He sounded friendly. Confident. Completely unthreatening.

She wasn't fooled for a second.

Her husband took over. "Good morning. We're from New Beginnings Church, and we—"

"Ah, yes, Molly told me you guys stopped by last weekend. Well, I appreciate your kindness, but we don't have any needs." Still smiling, he stepped back from the door. "You guys have a good day."

"Wait!" Lauren said, not liking the quiver in her voice. She tried to straighten it out. "I wanted to invite Molly to tea."

"I'm sorry?"

How could he have not heard her? Had she mumbled? She realized Roderick was looking at her with confusion. Maybe she had mumbled. She raised her voice, trying to be loud enough for Molly to hear—wherever she was. "I wanted to invite Molly to tea at the church. On Providence Ave." She sensed the husband was going to cut her off and started speaking faster, which for some reason made her louder as well. "Tomorrow at one o'clock. Don't need to bring anything! There will be tea and snacks! Dress is casual—"

"Thank you," he interrupted. "I think Molly might have plans tomorrow, but I'll let her know about your invitation."

She forced a smile. "Thank you."

He looked at her for just a second too long and then widened his smile. "Thanks for stopping by." And then the door was shut. With Molly still on the other side of it.

They were halfway back to the minivan before Roderick said, "*Tea party?*"

"I don't know," she admitted. "It's what came to my mind."

They climbed into the van. "You're spending too much time with our founders. You're turning into one of them." He snorted. "Tea party."

She didn't think turning out to be like those women would be a bad thing. "What was I supposed to do, invite her to go bar hopping?"

He laughed so heartily that she was encouraged. Maybe their fight was over. "Wouldn't take long to bar hop in Carver Harbor. Unless you're going to hop around inside the one bar."

She joined his laughter. "Aren't there two bars?"

"I'm not sure ... but a tea party?"

"It's all I could think of."

"But why did you think of anything? Did you go there planning to invite her to something?"

"A tea party?" Judith interrupted from the middle seat. "Can I go?"

"No," Mary Sue said, "because if you go, then I have to go to watch you."

"I don't need to be watched!" Judith cried with such confidence the statement almost seemed true.

"No," Lauren said. "I wasn't planning on anything. I wasn't really expecting him to answer the door, and when he did, I panicked. Didn't want to waste the opportunity, so I shouted out an invitation. Sorry. It probably wasn't my best moment."

"Nah. You were okay. But I don't think she'll go."

"I do."

He looked at her. "Why's that?"

"I think he'll make her go."

"What? That doesn't make any sense. If he's abusive, he's not going to want her to go hang out with a bunch of prying church women."

She hesitated, trying to figure out how to explain her hunch. "You are right in a way. I think a lot of abusive men keep their women hidden away, so that no one sees them and so that no one can give them strength. But did you see their yard?"

"What about it?"

"They obviously don't have a lot of money, yet the house and yard are neat and tidy. A rarity around here. And his truck was clean. No one washes their truck in January. Yet it was clean. And he was dressed sharply for a Saturday morning."

"I have no idea what you're trying to say."

She wasn't sure she did either. "I'm saying that this man cares what people think of him. So I think he'll make her go to tea. To keep up appearances."

Roderick sighed.

"Plus, he seemed a little cocky."

Roderick chuckled. "What does that have to do with anything?"

"Not sure. But if he's confident she won't ask for help, he'll be more likely to send her."

"Good grief. How much thought have you given this?"

She rubbed her forehead. "I haven't slept in days."

He sighed again. "Fine. You better talk to Rachel or Esther. You have to plan a tea party. And then, unless she ... *Molly* directly invites you to her house, we're not going back there."

Chapter 20

Chevon

Sick of sitting in the car, when they returned to deliver five pairs of winter boots, Chevon followed the others up to the door.

A woman answered the door and looked down at the Reny's bags dangling from Hype's arms. Her eyes grew wide.

"Would you like to try them on?" Cathy asked. "If they don't fit, we can go exchange them."

Quickly, as if she were afraid Hype might change his mind, the woman grabbed the bags from his hands. As she did so, Chevon clocked the giant iPhone in her right hand. "They'll fit, I'm sure. Thanks so much." The woman hesitated, as if trying to think of something else to say, but then apparently couldn't because she hurriedly thanked them again and shut the door.

Cathy sighed and turned away. "Come on, team. Let's go."

Chevon couldn't pinpoint what about that interaction had her so unsettled, but she knew she wasn't the only one. The very air in the car felt uneasy.

"Dude, her phone costs over a grand," Hype said.

"Yeah, I saw that," Chevon said.

"That was the newest model," Hype said. "It's only been out a week. And her son was wearing hundred-dollar high tops. I don't think they needed winter boots from Reny's."

"I recognized that kid," Jason chimed in. "I know him from helping coach the little kids. I don't think they're poor—"

"That's not for us to decide," Cathy said.

"Why not?" Hype said. "We just bought them boots!"

"*We* didn't buy them anything," Cathy said. "*God* bought them boots, and if she lied about a need, that's between her and God." She took a deep breath. "The Bible doesn't tell us to have people fill out applications and get sworn affidavits to prove how worthy they are of our help. The Bible tells us not to judge. To help. To be cheerful givers. The rest is up to God."

This philosophy made no sense. Chevon gave Jason a questioning look, but he only shrugged.

"So Christians," Chevon said. "They can just get manipulated and used and tricked and stolen from, and that's all okay with God?"

Cathy shook her head, and her flawless hair fell back into perfect place.

How on earth did she get her hair to behave so well?

"No. That's not okay with God, but it's up to him to deal with it, not us. And nobody can steal from me because nothing that I have is really my own. It all belongs to God. Especially since we literally took the money for those boots from his storehouse. Don't worry. God will not be mocked. No one ever gets away with anything. If that woman was dishonest, then she will have to account for that. But I don't think she meant to trick us. I don't think she thought we'd actually go get her boots. Maybe she was trying to get rid of us. Maybe she was testing us. I don't know. But I hope that our kindness taught her something about Christ's kindness."

This made some sense, but Chevon was reluctant to accept it as truth.

Apparently, so was Hype because he said, "You just used a lot of big words and you lost me, but I think it's simple. They didn't deserve our time, our help, or God's money."

"No, they didn't," Cathy said, which surprised Chevon. Cathy looked at her in the rearview. "But Jesus Christ died on the cross for me. I didn't deserve that time, that help, that gift. But I'm some grateful he gave it."

No one said anything, and a minute passed.

"Can I ask you guys for a favor?" Cathy asked.

Chevon was surprised by the question. She was even more surprised by how excited she was to do this woman a favor. The boys didn't answer, so Chevon said, "Sure."

"I stopped by a house last week, and I'm not passing judgment, but the mom was drunk. I'd like to stop there again and check on them."

Chevon waited for her to say more.

"So, what's the favor?" Hype asked.

"Well, last time she was quite obviously intoxicated. And she might be again today. I certainly hope not, but she might be. So the favor is, I'm asking you guys not to react. I don't want to embarrass anyone. But there were kids there. So I want to check on them."

Before any of them could answer, she parked in front of Katelynn's house.

"This house?" Chevon said.

"Yes." Cathy unbuckled her seatbelt.

"This is Katelynn's house."

Jason leaned over to look out Chevon's window. "Really?"

"Yes. Katelynn's mom was drunk?" She tried to picture Katelynn's mother but wasn't sure she'd ever seen her before.

"Maybe not. Maybe it wasn't her mother. But there was a drunk woman." She hesitated. "Maybe if you guys know this girl, you shouldn't come. I don't want to embarrass her."

"Okay," Jason and Hype said in unison.

"I'll come with you," Chevon said. "I won't be judgy. I promise."

Chapter 21

Esther

Esther was so exhausted she was cranky. Maybe she was too old for this. She wanted to be part of it all, but it was *a lot*. Maybe she should spearhead a prayer team that stayed behind and supported the teams in prayer.

Again, Walter, Levi, Zoe, and she had approached three houses. Again, no one had wanted their help. This time, two of the people had recognized Walter as the town lawyer and had made their dislike quite obvious. But it was unclear, to Esther at least, whether they disliked him for something he'd done while lawyering or simply because he was a lawyer.

Pastor Adam had a list of prayer requests that he'd collected around town, and as they prayed, Esther nearly dozed off. Maybe it *wouldn't* be prudent for her to spearhead the prayer team.

She was thankful when he said amen. She was trying to care about these people, some she knew, some she didn't, but she didn't have the energy. It was too hot in the sanctuary. Grateful for an excuse to move, she went to turn down the thermostat.

When she returned, Vicky glared at her. "Don't be a penny pincher. It's cold in here."

Esther sat down with a harrumph. "You just don't have any insulation." In the winter months, Esther was often grateful to wear an extra large.

"How did your team do?" Pastor asked Walter.

He reported their three strikes.

Then Tonya gave her summary. Someone needed new tires. Did anyone have any tires? No, but someone had a coupon for Tire Queen and was happy to give it away. Better than nothing. A retired man needed a ride to a doctor's appointment in Bangor. To no one's surprise, Dawn volunteered. Someone needed to buy their son a bus ticket home. Pastor declared that a worthy cause and sent Cathy to fetch the funds.

It was Nora's turn. Esther felt a pang of guilt for stealing Nora's son for her own team, but she'd made it clear Nora could join them, and she hadn't. So maybe she was trying to give her son some space to do his romancing. Nora reported some more prayer requests and then shared that one woman had offered the church her surplus of zucchini from the fall harvest.

"That's some old zucchini," Hype said.

"It was probably canned," Esther said.

Nora looked at her. "It was not."

Esther's stomach turned.

"All right," Pastor said, looking queasy. "Who's next?"

There was a steady stream of prayer requests. Sickness. Addiction. Pain. Estranged children. Cheating spouses. The longer they prayed, the more discouraged Esther got. This town was in worse shape than she'd thought. Were they even going to make a dent?

Then it was Lauren's turn. "You know that woman I told you about last week? I thought she was in need, but I wasn't sure about specifics." She took a long breath and looked right at Esther. "Well, I sort of invited her to a tea party. Here. Tomorrow. At one."

Vicky snickered.

"Are we hosting a tea party?" Pastor asked.

"We are now," Cathy said, sounding less than enthusiastic.

Lauren's face fell.

"I love tea!" Esther exclaimed and then winced. In trying to make up for Cathy's lack of verve, she had ended up sounding insane. She tried to tone it down. "No problem, Lauren. We can whip together a tea party, easy-peasy. Any ladies who can come, please bring any fun teas you have and any tea pots or teacups."

Nora looked bewildered. "I don't have any *fun* teas." She looked around. "Do people really drink fun tea?"

Levi chuckled. "It's okay, Mom. Some of us aren't the tea type."

"I don't think any of us are the tea type," Esther said before she knew what she was saying. "There's no such thing. It's just tea. It's just a beverage. It's something to drink. Something to do. An excuse to invite a woman within these walls." She smiled at Lauren. "And I think it's brilliant."

Walter gave her a precious smile. He looked proud of her.

She smiled back and then leaned over and whispered, "Want to take me shopping?"

Unsurprised, he nodded.

She leaned back. She didn't own any fancy tea equipment. And the only tea she had at home was Sleepytime. *Not* something she needed to be consuming in her present state.

After the meeting, she was in a hurry to leave, but Cathy beckoned her over to a huddle with Dawn and Vicky.

"What is it?" Esther tried to smash down her impatience.

"Remember that woman I told you about? The mother who'd been drinking?"

Esther didn't. All the town's sad stories had tangled themselves into one depressing mud patch in her head.

"Go on," Dawn said.

"Well, they didn't answer their door this time, even though it was clear people were home."

"How do you know people were home?" Dawn asked.

Cathy rolled her eyes. "I didn't have to be Columbo to figure it out. Smoke coming out of the chimney. Car in the yard. Kids shouting inside. All the lights were on."

"Maybe they didn't hear you knock," Vicky tried.

"They heard me."

"So what do you want to do?" Esther was in a hurry to get tea shopping.

"I want one or more of you to go back there with me. Right now."

"And do what?"

"I don't know. Try again."

"Why are you so worried about this woman again?" Dawn asked. "People drink, Cathy."

"I know that." Cathy's face grew red. "She ... she didn't look healthy. And it was eleven o'clock in the morning. And she had children. And her daughter was obviously covering for her. As if she'd done it a million times before. As if she were used to having a drunken mother."

"I still don't know what we can do." Dawn pursed her lips.

"I could talk to Katelynn," a young voice said from behind her.

Esther turned to see Chevon and stepped aside to let her into the huddle.

"Sorry, didn't mean to eavesdrop. But I could talk to Katelynn at school on Monday."

No one answered her.

Chevon grew visibly agitated. "Look, if you don't want my help, just say so, but I'm pretty sure I can talk to another teenager without screwing this up."

"No, no," Cathy said quickly. "You won't screw it up. I know that. You'll do just fine. Thank you." She smiled, and Esther noticed that she too looked exhausted. "Will you let me know how it goes? I don't want to lose more sleep than I have to."

Chevon's face grew serious. "Sure. I can text you."

Chapter 22

Lauren

Lauren loved Pastor Adam, but his preaching left a lot to be desired. She wondered if he'd let her write him an outline. He needed a beginning and an end. With a straight line connecting the two. Sure, he'd probably still get off track, but at least he'd be able to look down and see that connecting line.

She glanced at the time and then at the door. Roderick caught her looking and seemed annoyed. It was at least the hundredth time she'd looked at the door, and her looking didn't even make sense. She'd invited Molly to a one o'clock tea party, not to the church service before. She had no reason to show up two hours early.

She had no reason to show up at all.

Lauren sighed and tried to focus on Pastor's words, which were jumbled. He was now talking about Jeremiah, but she was pretty sure he still meant Joshua. She didn't think Jeremiah had ever crossed the Jordan, and if he had, it hadn't been a big deal.

Finally, the church service was over, and Lauren found herself mentally pushing her brothers and sisters out of the sanctuary. People had a tendency to linger, jibber-jabbering. She glanced at the time again. They had nearly an hour. Plenty of time for jibber-jabber. She noticed Esther and Zoe struggling with a folded table. Well, Esther was struggling, not Zoe. Lauren hurried to help.

"Thank you," Esther said.

"No, thank *you*. Thanks for helping me with this crazy scheme and for making it seem less crazy."

"It's not crazy at all." Esther glanced at the organ. "This isn't the first time we've used tea to try to lure someone in."

Zoe laughed.

Esther looked at her sharply. "What's so funny?"

"Don't use the word *lure*, Gramma. It makes us sound evil."

Esther pressed her lips together. "You're right. I s'pose it does. I don't know what other word to use, though, that means trying to get people into the church."

"Lately, we've been trying to take the church to the people," Lauren said.

"You're right," Esther said. "And that's a good thing."

Vicky appeared with a pastel purple plastic tablecloth, and Rachel was right behind her with a huge colorful bouquet.

"Looks like you guys have this under control," Zoe said. "I'm going home."

"You're not staying?" Lauren said.

"Um ... no."

Lauren looked around the sanctuary for her own daughter. She had hoped Mary Sue would stay, but it seemed her whole family had left her. She sighed. She needed to help Molly and then focus on not annoying her husband. She hadn't meant to get so far off track with him.

Her eyes returned to the table, where plates of cookies and cupcakes had appeared, as well as two fairly exquisite teacup and tea pot sets. Where had those come from? The table looked amazing, but it was also full. "Where are people going to sit?"

"Here." Rachel pushed a plush wing chair toward them and then stood up and mopped her brow.

"Good idea," Lauren said and went to get another.

Soon they had a small circle of relatively comfortable, if mismatched, furniture near the table. Church members had filtered out. The water was boiled.

And eight women stood or sat around, quietly waiting.

"Who are we waiting for again?" Vera squinted at Esther.

Esther glanced at the clock. In seconds it would be one o'clock. "Just waiting till the official start time," Esther said.

And then the official start time came, and most of them still stared at the door—which slowly swung open to reveal a well put-together young woman with a timid look on her face.

Cathy rushed to the door. "Welcome!"

The scared look on Molly's face prodded Lauren into action, and she followed after Cathy. "Hi, Molly! Welcome!" She swept an arm toward the table of goodies. "I'm so glad you made it. Come on in, and I'll introduce you to people."

Molly took two steps and stopped.

"Can I hang your coat up for you?" Cathy asked.

"No thanks," Molly said softly, but she did take her coat off. Then she followed Lauren toward the comfy chairs.

"Hi, Molly," Rachel said as she poured water into a tea pot. "Sorry, we're running a bit behind. Just getting these teas steeping right now."

If Molly hadn't shown up, would they have had tea at all?

Chapter 23

Lauren

Molly held a teacup with two small lemon cookies balanced on the saucer. Lauren could smell the lemon—whether it was from the cookies or the lemon wedges some hospitable sister had cut up, she didn't know, but it was making her mouth water. But she avoided eating anything as she wanted to be social and not have her mouth full while trying to befriend this woman.

"I'm so glad you could come," she said awkwardly. This was a variance of something she'd already said twice. She hurried to improve. "I'm a little surprised." Then she winced. Had that been rude?

Molly smiled and exhaled. "Yeah, me too." She took a sip of her tea.

Lauren laughed, probably too dramatically, but Molly didn't seem to mind. Her brain searched for words. "I know that being invited to church can make you want to run for the hills, but we're one of the good ones." Molly didn't say anything, and Lauren felt pressure to keep talking. "Not that there are bad ones, but ..." She stopped. How was she so terrible at this?

Molly looked at her out of the corner of her eye. "I watch the news. I'm pretty sure there are bad ones."

Relieved, Lauren laughed again. "Absolutely. I just felt guilty saying so."

Molly giggled, and Lauren was greatly encouraged.

"I say that I mostly come to church for my kids, but these women are amazing. I love knowing them. They've enriched my life so much."

Molly's eyes scanned the room. She didn't look skeptical. She took another sip of tea.

"Do you have any kids?"

She shook her head and looked down. "No. Not yet."

"Well, you're young yet. Plenty of time."

Molly looked at her and smiled. "I'm not that young."

Lauren didn't know what to say to that, so she changed the subject. "Are you from around here?"

Molly nodded. "Born and raised."

"Cool! Do you have family in the area? Nieces or nephews?"

Her face became impassive. "I did, but ... my family was small, and we lost touch years ago."

"Oh. That's sad. Do they live locally?"

She shrugged. "There is no *they*, I don't think. My parents died, and I've only got one sister. She has a few kids, but ... like I said, we don't talk, and I don't know where she lives now. It's probably still somewhere close, but ..." Her voice trailed off as she looked thoughtful. "She was never very adventurous, so I think she's probably in Maine, but it doesn't really matter, as we don't—"

"Who's not very adventurous?" Vicky dragged a cushioned chair closer.

Molly looked alarmed.

Under other circumstances, Lauren would have been annoyed at someone eavesdropping and then crashing her conversation, but she was relieved to have help.

Molly didn't answer.

"Molly's sister."

"Ah! You're estranged?"

Molly furrowed her brow. "I guess."

"What'd she do?"

Lauren flinched. That was pushing a little too hard, wasn't it?

Molly didn't appear to be offended. "It was all a long time ago, but she ... let's just say I couldn't really trust her around my husband, and then fighting over that led to fighting over lots of things, and we basically just decided to hate each other."

Vicky chuckled humorlessly. "Sometimes that does seem the easiest route to take."

"Yeah, but I sure do miss her."

"So how long have you been married?" Vicky asked quickly.

Molly looked down at her almost-empty teacup.

Yes, definitely, there was something wrong here. "Almost ten years. But we've been together longer." She smiled, but it looked strained.

"What does he do?" Vicky asked.

"He's a lineman."

"Oh wow! That's a great job. Does he have to travel a lot?"

"Not really. Sometimes."

"Well, if you're ever lonely while he's gone, don't be." Lauren looked at the other ladies. "We're always here."

"Thank you." She sounded sincere.

"Do you work outside the home?" Vicky asked.

Molly shook her head. "I have health issues. Can't really work."

Lauren's chest tightened. Health issues. Of course.

"What kind of health issues?"

Wow. Good thing Vicky had shown up. She was not worried one bit about being polite.

"I get bad headaches. They lay me up for days."

"I'm so sorry to hear that. Next time that happens, let us know, and we'll bring you some meals so you can rest—"

"Oh no, that's all right. Trevor takes good care of me when I'm like that."

"That's good to hear," Vicky said slowly. "But when it happens while he's away at work, he can't be much help."

Molly smiled and leaned forward in her chair. "I think I should be going."

Shoot. Vicky had pressed too hard.

"Hang on just a second." Vicky also scooted forward in her seat. "Lauren, write her a list of our phone numbers so she can find us if she needs us."

"That isn't necessary—" Molly tried.

"Nonsense. It doesn't hurt to have resources. No one is saying you have to use them."

Of course, Lauren had no pen or paper, and she didn't know why Vicky had assumed she would be prepared to whip up a list on command. "Hang on, Molly. Let me go find a pen." She practically ran to the office, where she found two broken pencils and a thick, black permanent marker. Good grief. She ripped open drawer after drawer to no avail.

Finally she gave up and grabbed the marker. She would just have to explain that it was all she could find and that she wasn't trying to be aggressive with her ink choice. She wrote down her name and number and then scrolled through her phone to add

Vicky's, Rachel's, and Pastor Adam's. Then she hurried back out into the sanctuary to find Vicky standing right where she'd left her—alone.

"Sorry. She was in a hurry to leave."

Lauren dropped her arms to her side. "Shoot." It occurred to her to be annoyed with Vicky, but Vicky had done a better job of engaging Molly than she had.

"You're right. Something isn't right there."

Relief flooded through her. "I know."

"We need to be praying."

"Yes, we do."

Chapter 24

Chevon

Chevon lay awake on Sunday night, her brain spinning. A million thoughts competed for her attention, and no amount of tossing or turning could slow them down.

Oddly, among swirling stressful thoughts about baby and Jason, an image of that stupid cat kept taking center stage. How could she have been so stupid to invest herself in some crazy old lady's long dead cat? She was such a moron. Or maybe not. Maybe there was still hope. As annoyed as she was with Fanny, her heart also broke along with hers. She couldn't imagine losing a pet and not knowing what had happened to him. But what if she were a weird old lady living all alone and *then* losing a cat and not knowing what happened to him? It would be torture.

And that's what it was. Torture. Grief. A horrible story with no happy ending possible. No hope. This thought made her feel guilty. Maybe there was still hope. If that cat were out there somewhere, then surely she should still hope it came home. Even if it took a miracle.

Miracle. She was starting to think like the Christians Jason was forcing her to hang around. Jason, who didn't think God cared about cats. The thought made her grind her teeth in annoyance. How she wished she could prove him wrong on that one. Chevon didn't know much about God, but she did know that if he existed, if he really did create all the creatures on the earth, then surely he cared about them.

How she wished God would prove her right by proving that love to Jason.

Maybe she should pray about it. The idea startled her. Pray? Her? She didn't know how. Wait, that wasn't true. Of course she knew how. She'd been listening to people pray—all the time—for weeks.

She could do this. She tried to focus, tried to calm her thoughts. This was harder than she'd expected. Her thoughts wouldn't stop, but at least they slowed down. *Hi, God*, she thought, and then nearly giggled. *You probably weren't expecting to hear from me.* Or maybe he was. If he was the all-knowing God that those people claimed him to be, then he'd known since the beginning of time that she was going to pray this prayer right this second. This thought freaked her out, made her feel impossibly small, and she shook it out of her head, focusing instead on what she was going to say next. *I was wondering if you could bring that cat back. I know it's kind of impossible. The cat is probably dead. And I'm not asking you to bring a dead cat back. That would be way too Stephen King.* She paused. Would God understand Stephen King references? Probably, right? If he could read her mind, and the only way he could hear this prayer right now is if he could read her mind, then certainly he could put the reference together. Ugh. Here she was again, thoughts spinning aimlessly. She squeezed her eyes shut. *Anyway, I just wanted to ask you to bring the cat home. Not for me, but for Fanny.* This was kind of a lie. *Well, mostly for Fanny.* There. Prayer finished. Now what? She didn't really understand the whole "in Jesus' name" thing, so she just said, "Amen." The whisper felt loud in her quiet room, and she jumped. Just what she needed—a rush of adrenaline at two in the morning. *Oh, and one more thing, please. Could you please help me fall asleep?*

Chevon's alarm went off, and she groped around on her nightstand. Her fingers found her phone and hit snooze. She tried to fall back asleep, but her bladder wouldn't let her, so she swung her legs out of bed. She rubbed her eyes and looked at the clock. Wow, she'd actually gotten a few hours of uninterrupted sleep. What a miracle. She stopped. Had it been a miracle? Had God made her fall asleep because she'd asked him to? No way.

If so, then she needed to start praying every night as soon as she lay down, not wait till the 2 a.m. desperation set in. She laughed at the thought. Whether God had put her to sleep or not, she was going to start praying before bed, for sure.

Chapter 25

Chevon

Holding her lunch tray out in front of her, Chevon turned to face the cafeteria. She usually didn't have to think about where she was going to sit. She just sat with Jason, Hype, Levi, and Zoe.

But she was looking for Katelynn.

Where on earth was she? She scanned each table. Someone bumped into her elbow as she stood there.

"Yeah, no problem. You're excused," she said loudly.

She looked at the line behind her. No Katelynn. Was she even in school today?

She headed toward her usual table. "Do you guys know if Katelynn is in school today?"

They all looked up at her. "Who?" Jason asked.

"Katelynn."

His face remained blank.

"Katelynn Stanley. We were at her house two days ago?"

"Why are you looking for her?"

His ignorance gave her a little thrill. *She* had a secret with the church folk. Those people squarely belonged to Jason and Zoe, yet *she* had a secret with them. She knew this delight she was taking was absurd, and still—she allowed it.

"None of your business. Have any of you seen her today?"

Obviously offended, Jason turned his attention to his tater tots.

"Sorry, I don't know if she's here," Zoe said. "I'm too self-absorbed to notice others' attendance."

Hype chuckled. "I'm not self-absorbed, but I don't know either. You should ask her friends."

Chevon looked up. She didn't know who Katelynn's friends were. Did she have any? She tried to remember seeing Katelynn hanging out with someone, or even talking to someone, but she couldn't. She looked at Hype. "Good idea. Who are her friends?"

He finished a swig of his milk, giving himself a small milk mustache that made Chevon's stomach roll. She put her tray down, her appetite gone. Without looking at him and his mustache, she explained, "You said to ask her friends. Who do you mean? Who does she hang out with?"

He was quiet for so long that she had to look at him.

He was scanning the cafeteria. "I think she's in band?"

Great. Chevon had no idea who else was in band. This was ridiculous. She walked purposefully to the nearest table. "Do any of you know where Katelynn is?"

"Who?"

What? Was this girl invisible?

"Katelynn."

"What do you want with Katelynn?" He actually managed to sound protective of her.

"Oh for crying out loud. Do you know where she is or not?"

"She usually eats in the art room," someone else said sheepishly.

The art room? They were allowed to eat in the art room? She left the cafeteria and weaved her way to the art room. The smell of paint and clay wafted out at her and made her stomach roll again. Good grief. She needed to get some nose plugs for school.

The door to the art room was closed, and she peeked in through the window, but saw no one. She slowly opened the door, and the scents grew stronger. Ugh. If this made her throw up, she was going to be angry. She took a few steps and heard voices.

The art teacher. And someone else. Probably Katelynn. She crept closer until she could peek into the art teacher's office. Yes, Katelynn was in there. Katelynn had lunch in the art teacher's office? How bizarre. She backed up toward the door, and her hip—which she swore now stuck out farther than it had a week ago—knocked a paintbrush off the end of a table.

Chevon couldn't believe how much noise a paintbrush could make. She turned to scurry out of the room, but it was too late. "Can I help you?"

Ugh. She didn't know this teacher, and this teacher didn't know her. She looked over her shoulder. "No, sorry, just looking for someone." Then she got out of there as fast as she could.

I'm pretty sure I can handle talking to a girl at school, she'd told Cathy. And now she was proving that might not be the case.

She groaned and headed back to the cafeteria.

"Did you find her?" Levi asked.

"Sort of."

"What's that mean?" Jason asked.

"Did you know you can eat lunch in the art room?"

Hype shook his head slowly. "I don't think that's true. Besides, why would you want to? Mrs. Movack is terrifying. And I think all she eats are vegetables. She would probably make you eat bean sprouts for lunch."

Chapter 26

Chevon

Though she had forgotten about looking for her, Chevon spotted Katelynn standing in line for the bus. She changed course to head that way. "Hey, Katelynn. Want a ride home?"

Katelynn looked bewildered. "What? Why?"

The boy in front of her in line snickered, and Chevon considered planting her boot in his butt.

"No reason. I just know riding the bus is no picnic. I thought you might like a ride."

Katelynn continued to look suspicious, but she also apparently really hated riding the school bus because she nodded. "Okay. Sure. Why not?"

"Awesome." *Don't sound too excited*, Chevon told herself. She walked slowly to her car, as if Katelynn might lose her.

She started the engine and cranked the heat. "Want to stop and get a soda or something?"

Katelynn squeezed her brows together. "Were you in the art room today?"

Busted. "Yeah, so let's go get a soda." She backed out of a parking spot, trying to think quickly. It was only a two-minute drive to Katelynn's house, maybe five with the soda stop. She had to get this thing going.

"So not to be weird or anything, but I was just a little bit worried about you. Are you doing okay?"

Katelynn leaned away from her a few inches. "Are you like a pregnant lesbian now?"

Chevon laughed, but when she looked at Katelynn's eyes, there was no hint of humor there. Had that been Katelynn's version of mean? "No. I mean, yes to the pregnant, no to the lesbian."

Katelynn continued to study her. "So, what? You're like hard up for friends now?"

Yes, she was trying to be mean. Which was really strange. Chevon had never heard her utter a mean word. But Katelynn's barb did no damage. Even though it wasn't far from the truth, it didn't hurt. Chevon was beyond caring about stuff like that. This realization brought her a surge of joy. It felt good to be free. "Nah. I have enough friends, but I wouldn't mind one more."

Katelynn's body relaxed a little. "You're weird."

Chevon laughed again. "Aren't we all?"

She chuckled. "I guess." She looked out her window, and it was nice to be relieved of her intense gaze.

Chevon pulled into the gas station.

"What are we doing here?"

"I told you I would buy you a soda. What kind do you want?"

"Can't I go in?"

"Of course."

Katelynn wanted to be a part of the soda shopping. This was great news.

Katelynn followed her to the store, and they both went to the soda fountain. Chevon held her cup under the ginger ale tap.

"Ginger ale? That's so boring. What are you, an old lady?"

Chevon laughed. "It is boring. I used to be a Dr. Pepper girl, but" — she rubbed her belly — "no caffeine for a few months."

"Longer than that. Unless you're not going to breastfeed."

Her words surprised Chevon. She hadn't expected such an aware comment.

"Yeah, I'm trying not to think about that part. The whole thing freaks me out. You've got some younger siblings?"

Katelynn ignored the baiting question, and Chevon realized that she had moved from the Cherry Coke to the Sprite. As she watched, Katelynn moved on to grape.

"What are you doing?"

Katelynn shrugged. "Variety is the spice of life."

"That's disgusting."

She laughed.

"You're the weirdo."

Katelynn laughed again, and it sounded so sincere that an excitement filled Chevon from head to toe. She had made a new friend, and it hadn't even been that hard.

When they got back in the car, Katelynn said, "So for real. Why are you being nice to me all of a sudden? I mean, you've never been *mean* to me, but not that long ago you wouldn't have been caught dead with me in public."

This was an exaggeration, but Chevon took her point.

"In a lot of ways I have more anxiety than I've ever had before, but in a lot of other categories, I could not possibly care less. I can't believe I ever cared about that stuff at all. I guess I've changed a lot." She pulled her car out onto the street.

"You mean like basketball?"

"Yes, like basketball."

"And following Alita around?"

She didn't think she had ever followed Alita around. At least she certainly hoped not. And she hated that it might have appeared like that to others. "Yeah. Alita wants me dead."

Katelynn laughed. "Yeah, well I guess we have something in common then."

Chevon looked at her sharply. "Why would Alita hate you?"

"Why wouldn't she? She thinks I'm trash. But more importantly, she tried to cheat off me in sixth grade and I ratted her out, and she got in trouble."

Chevon laughed so suddenly that ginger ale almost came out her nose. Once she got control of her faculties, she asked, "Are you serious? She might want to get over that by now."

"You know Alita."

Yes, yes, she did. She wanted to ask more questions, but she was out of time. And suddenly it was more important to her that Katelynn liked and trusted her than her getting her info.

"Thanks for the ride." Katelynn grabbed her bag and got out of the car. "And the soda."

"You bet. Anytime." Chevon looked past her, at her house, looking for signs of anything amiss.

"What are you looking at?"

Chevon pulled her eyes back to Katelynn, who looked suspicious.

"Oh nothing. Just staring off into space. See you tomorrow."

She seemed to accept that explanation. "Yeah, okay. Thanks again." She shut the car door, and Chevon pulled out her phone.

"I didn't learn anything," she texted to Cathy. "But I made a new friend, so that's cool."

Cathy answered immediately. "That's better than cool, honey. Great job."

Chevon drove away, beaming with satisfaction at that tidbit of praise.

Chapter 27

Esther

Esther put down her knitting to answer her phone, something she wouldn't have done if it weren't Walter on the other end of the call. Or maybe Zoe.

"Hullo?"

"Hello, beautiful."

Esther's heart swelled.

"I was wondering if you wanted to go ride around town looking for Derek."

"Why, what's wrong?"

"Nothing's wrong, that I know of, but I haven't made my offer to him yet. I haven't even seen him."

"Wasn't he in church yesterday?" As she said the words, she realized the answer. No, he hadn't been. "Is he even in town?"

"No idea."

She started to worry. Not that something was wrong, necessarily. She had complete faith that Derek could keep himself alive. She was worried he'd vanished and she wasn't going to see him again. He freaked her out, even scared her a little, but she'd also grown quite fond of him. He was becoming like family.

"But it's going to be cold tonight, so I thought I'd go look."

"Sure. It's a nice night for a drive. Come pick me up."

He was there so quickly Esther wondered if he'd called from the lobby downstairs. She quickly checked her hair and teeth in the mirror and then silently chided herself for doing so. Don't be silly, she thought.

He held the door open for her, and she led him to the elevator. Her neighbor Milton, who she was starting to think just rode the elevator up and down for fun, looked Walter up and down with a critical eye.

Walter ignored him.

"Have a nice evening, Milton," Esther said as she stepped off onto the main floor.

"I think that man is sweet on you," Walter said as they stepped outside.

Esther laughed shrilly. "Don't be ridiculous." The theory was just that: ridiculous. Yet Esther still loved that Walter had spoken it.

They started driving.

"Probably should have done this before dusk."

"Maybe," Esther said, not wanting to agree with his self-criticism, "but who knows?"

"I don't even know where to check. The bars?"

"I don't think he can afford to drink at a bar."

"Good point. Then where?"

"I don't know. Have you checked with Pastor?"

"I did. He hasn't seen him. Neither has Roderick."

"Shoot." Esther racked her brain but came up empty.

They continued driving in circles, and though they weren't accomplishing much, Esther was enjoying Walter's company.

When they were headed north on Main Street for the third time, Walter said, "He must be indoors somewhere. So where in Carver Harbor might he be indoors?"

"If he's in someone's house, we'll never find him."

"If he's in someone's house, we don't need to find him." Walter chuckled ruefully. "Unless he's there uninvited."

"I don't think he'd do that." She didn't know that for sure, though.

"What about a business? What business would let Derek hang out inside?"

She couldn't think of any. "All I can think of is a church." She hated that they wouldn't let him hang out at New Beginnings.

"I know how you feel about that, Esther, but it's just not possible right now. And it's silly to heat a whole building for one man."

Maybe. Maybe not. "Wait!" Esther cried.

Walter stepped on the brake. "What?"

"The laundromat." They'd just driven by.

"What, did you see him?"

"No, I didn't see anyone, but I saw the laundromat, and that seems like a place that would let him in. There's usually no one there to kick him out."

"All right. Let's go back and check." He pulled over to the curb and then did a U-turn in the road.

"Gee whiz, act like you own the whole town, why don't you?"

Walter looked at her out of the corner of his eye. "Esther, are you flirting with me?"

"Who me? Never!"

He pulled into the laundromat. "This was a great theory. If he isn't hanging out here, then he should be. You want to go in with me?"

She basked in his praise. "No thanks. I'll let you do the honors."

He laughed and climbed out into the cold, turning his collar up against the ocean wind. In most parts of the world, such oceanfront property wouldn't be dedicated to a laundromat, but here in Carver Harbor, people took ocean views for granted.

Seconds later, Walter came back out of the laundromat with Derek right behind him. Derek had a giant backpack slung over his shoulder. It probably contained everything he owned. He never had it in church, though, making Esther wonder where he stashed it when he came to Providence Ave.

Derek climbed into the back, carrying the scent of alcohol with him. "Howdy, Miss Esther!"

"Hi, Derek." She mostly trusted him, but she didn't like having her back to him, especially if he'd been drinking. She silently prayed for protection and peace.

Once Walter had returned to his spot behind the wheel, Derek said, "So what's this burning question you wanted to ask me?"

"First, do you need anything to eat?"

"Nah," Derek said quickly. "The church feeds me. What is it?" He wasn't enjoying the dramatic suspense.

Walter turned in his seat to look into the backseat. The lights from the laundromat lit the interior of the car.

"I was thinking," Walter began. He sounded nervous. "I live alone in a big house, and I was wondering if you might want to stay in my guest room for a while?"

At first Derek said nothing. Then, "As in sleep there?"

"Yes. Sleep there. Have you been sleeping in the laundromat?"

Unsurprisingly, he did not answer this. "What's the catch?"

"No catch," Walter said quickly. "I would ask that you don't drink or be drunk in my house—"

"I don't drink," he said quickly.

Esther was certain this wasn't true.

"Perfect. I would ask that you would be respectful and not cause any harm to me or my property. But other than that, you can use the room, come and go as you please. It has its own bathroom."

Derek audibly gasped. "Does it have a tub?"

Walter nodded. "It has a tub." Walter gave him a minute, but Derek didn't say anything. "So is that a yes?"

Still nothing. Then, "Yes, that's a yes." His voice was shaking. He was obviously crying. Esther was glad she wasn't looking at him.

"Great." Walter put the car in reverse and backed up. "You okay to go there now?"

"Yes. Thank you." After a long silence, he asked, "Why are you doing this for me?"

It seemed Walter was prepared for this question. "Because Jesus would do it for me."

Chapter 28

Lauren

"Lauren!" Vicky cried, sounding delighted. "How did you get away?"

It was Lauren's first Tuesday morning prayer meeting. Roderick frequently came, when work would allow it, but Lauren could never manage to get away from the kids. "Not sure." She sank into a folding metal chair. "I mentioned I might like to go, and Roderick offered to take the kids."

"You've got yourself a good man, there," Barbara said.

This was true. "I know. Thank you for saying so."

A few more people straggled in as Pastor welcomed them all to the meeting. When he opened the floor to prayer requests, Lauren tried to let someone else go first but then couldn't stand it. "Can we pray for Molly?"

"Of course." Pastor wrote something down in his notebook. "Remind me who Molly is?"

This annoyed Lauren. She opened her mouth to remind him, but Vicky cut her off.

"The abused woman that we've been praying for."

Pastor looked confused, but he said, "Oh."

Lauren thought Vicky's bold labeling would attract some attention from the others in the circle, but it didn't. Apparently they were all absorbed in their own prayer requests.

The list grew and grew, and Lauren looked at the clock. Prayer was invaluable and shouldn't be rushed, but man, it was almost lunch time. Finally, Pastor suggested they start praying.

Vicky took up the mantle for her. "Father, we lift up precious Molly. We are not sure what's going on with her, but we can see something isn't right. We ask you to protect her and to bring her closer to yourself. And please give us wisdom in how to best minister to her. Thank you."

Someone else started praying, and Lauren realized she was disappointed. It had been a fine prayer. Vicky was good at praying. And yet she was left wanting. What had she expected? She didn't know. But that wasn't enough.

Still thinking about Molly, she had trouble focusing on or caring about any of the other things people were sharing. She felt a little guilty about this, but that guilt wasn't enough to make her care.

When they were done praying, Pastor smiled broadly. "Thanks for coming, everyone. It might not feel like it, but we moved mountains today."

"Wait," Lauren said as everyone started to get up.

Most of them sat back down.

"Can we ... I don't know what needs to be done, but can we do more for Molly?"

Vicky didn't look surprised. "We've got to be careful not to scare her off. Or alarm her husband into not letting us see her."

"Why *did* he let her come to that tea?" Barbara asked. "If he's abusive, wouldn't he want to keep her from us?"

"Not necessarily," Lauren said. "Sometimes they want to dangle their victims right in front of people who want to help, as if to say, I know you know, but there's nothing you can do about it."

No one said anything, and Lauren grew self-conscious. Maybe she shouldn't say things like that in settings like these.

"I could bake her a pie?" Esther said.

"That's a great idea!" Rachel said. "Esther will bake her a pie, and then you and Vicky can deliver it."

"When?" Vicky crowed. "I have a doctor's appointment this afternoon."

Esther shrugged. "Tomorrow morning, then. What kind do you think she'd like?"

Lauren had no idea. "I don't know. Whatever you'd like to make."

"Perfect. I'll make blackberry. I've got a bunch in the freezer."

"Thank you," Lauren said.

Pastor dismissed them again and then came up to Lauren. "Got a minute?"

Actually, she wanted to get home, but he was the pastor. "Sure."

"I love your heart for this woman, but I want to make sure that you are safe."

What? "Of course I'm safe."

"Sometimes we can get too invested in other people's pain, and it ends up causing more—"

"I'm fine," she interrupted, beyond annoyed. "I'm not too invested. I just want to make sure she's okay."

He stared at her for several seconds. "Okay then. You have a good day. Say hi to Roderick."

"I will." She zipped up her coat. "Thank you." She headed for the door. Had she been too snippy with him? Maybe. Oh well, it was too late now. And all these well-meaning people thinking she was overreacting? They didn't understand. They didn't know what she knew.

Chapter 29

Chevon

After school Chevon found Katelynn in the bus line again. "You want a ride?" she called from thirty feet away.

Looking surprised, Katelynn stepped out of line and headed her way. When she'd snapped her seatbelt into place, she said, "So I know Jason DeGrave is a religious nut now. Are you a religious nut too? Is that what this is? Am I a religious project?"

She was back to sounding mean. Shoot. Chevon had thought they were past this. "No. You are not a project. And I don't even believe in any of that religious stuff."

Katelynn laughed coldly. "I feel for you then, dating a religious nut when you know better."

Chevon didn't like the direction of this conversation. She was feeling defensive of Jason. And maybe even his church too. "It's not so bad." Then she remembered Jason preaching at her about being yoked together and she didn't feel as defensive. She'd looked that stuff up online and had learned the Bible was talking about oxen. Basically her husband-to-be had called her an ox.

"Ironic, isn't it? Jason DeGrave finds Jesus, becomes a religious fanatic, and then gets a girl pregnant?" She snickered. "Not the order of events someone might expect."

"He's not a religious fanatic. He believes in God, and I admire his faith. It takes a lot of courage to make the changes he's made."

"Sorry, sorry. Don't need to get all defensive."

Chevon tried to act as though Katelynn's accusations weren't bothering her. Maybe she didn't want to be friends with this person after all.

"Want a soda? It's my turn to treat."

Actually, a ginger ale did sound good. "Sure. Thanks." She pulled her car in the gas station parking lot.

"Want to live on the edge? I can make you my special recipe."

Chevon laughed. "No thanks."

Chevon got her boring old ginger ale, and Katelynn loaded up with a bit of everything. When they returned to the car, Katelynn took a long gulp and then said, "I don't really want to go home yet. Can we just sit here for a minute?"

"Of course. Anywhere else you want to go?"

She shook her head slowly. "I don't have much time. My brothers and sisters will be home soon. I just don't want to beat them there."

Chevon didn't understand what she meant. "I would think it would be nice having the house be a little quieter."

Katelynn let out a guttural laugh. "Oh, my house is rarely quiet, and when it is, that's when I really need to worry."

What? What was she talking about? "Everything okay?"

Katelynn looked at her and squinted. "Are you sure I'm not a religious project?"

"I'm sure."

She took a long breath. "Yeah. Things are okay. But only because I hold everything together. But that's okay too. I don't even usually mind. But it's a lot."

"Why do you have to hold things together?"

She shrugged. "My mom has issues. It's not her fault. My dad's gone. So I take care of my brothers and sisters."

Shoot. Cathy had been right. "That's a lot for a teenager. I'm freaking out about having a single baby, and you've got multiple."

She laughed sincerely. "Yes, but all of mine are potty trained."

They laughed together. Chevon started the car. "Let's go down to the lighthouse, see what we can see."

"Okay, but don't get too far from my house. I really don't have much time."

"So what would happen if they were home for a while with your mom?" Would she abuse them?

"Maybe nothing. Maybe something. It depends on what mood my mom is in."

This told Chevon exactly nothing. "Katelynn, I don't want to be nosy, but—"

"But you're about to be?" She laughed.

"Maybe a little. But if things are that bad, you could get some help. You could call—"

"I can't call anyone. We don't have any family to help. I used to have an aunt, but she took off, and something happened to make my mom hate her. I was little, and I don't remember." She sounded so sad.

"I'm sorry. But I meant you could call the state."

"No *way*," she said emphatically. "If someone calls the state, my mom will get in trouble, and we kids will be split up, so that's out of the question. And I've heard that once that process starts, it's impossible to stop. So please don't say anything. It's not like it's that bad anyway. As soon as I graduate, I'll get a job and then take care of all of them, and it will be much easier."

From zero information to an overwhelming onslaught. "Who told you that?"

"Told me what?"

"That they would split you up?"

"My mom."

Tread carefully, she thought. She wished Cathy were there. "So your mom has some issues, but she told you not to tell anybody, because the state would come and split you guys up? That sounds a tad manipulative."

Katelynn looked at her sharply. "You don't understand."

"You're right. I don't. I'm sorry. I wasn't trying to pretend that I do. I just want to help."

"Why do you want to help?"

Chevon shrugged. "I don't know. Feels good to worry about someone else's problems instead of mine."

"That sounds legitimate." The lighthouse came into view. "I'm not much for scenery. Can you take me home?"

"Of course." Chevon turned the car around. She took a different road to cut across the peninsula to Katelynn's house. A cardboard sign driven into the snowbank made her hit the brakes.

"What is it?"

"That sign said free kittens."

"So? Are you in the market for a free kitten?"

"No, but I know someone who might be." Chevon backed up the street and stopped in front of the sign, looking at the house, trying to evaluate how creepy it was.

"Aren't kittens usually born in spring?" Katelynn asked.

"No idea." Chevon unbuckled and looked at Katelynn. "You want to come with me?"

"Not really, but I will."

Tentatively, the two girls approached the front door.

Chevon knocked, and a harried-looking woman opened the door. She looked them up and down and said, "Are you from that church?"

"What church?" Katelynn asked.

Chevon had a pretty good idea what church she meant. "No, we're not from any church. We saw your kitten sign."

The woman's eyes grew wide. "Oh, come on in!" She ushered them inside and shut the door behind them.

Immediately, Katelynn sneezed.

"Bless you." Chevon scanned the room as her eyes adjusted to the lack of light. She counted five cats. No kittens.

"We just put that sign out. I didn't expect it to do much."

"You should put an ad in Uncle Henry's." Katelynn sneezed again.

"I did."

"Isn't it a little late in the year for kittens?" Katelynn asked.

She didn't answer. "Come into the kitchen."

Katelynn sneezed again, and Chevon grew scared she was going to leave. She was beyond glad that Katelynn was there with her. She wasn't sure she could manage this on her own.

The kitchen was full of cats.

The woman swung her arm across the room. "Go ahead. Take your pick."

Chevon looked at her, incredulous. "Are you serious?"

"Absolutely. I hate to let any of them go, but my husband says I have to cut back or he's going to take some of them out into the woods and drop them off."

Chevon wished she could take a carload of them. But she was walking on thin ice with her father already, and a single cat might push him over the edge. She looked at the cats, unsure how to proceed. "What about the kittens? These all look old."

The woman laughed. "Yes, some of these are kittens. A few months old."

"A few months?" Katelynn said. "They're huge."

"Well you don't have to take any. I didn't ask you to come knock on my door."

"No, no," Chevon said quickly. "I do want a kitten. Could you just point out which are the young ones?"

The woman looked at her like she was stupid, but she did as she was asked, pointing out the young ones one by one. As she did so, an orange tabby came and rubbed against Chevon's leg. She looked down at him. "Is he small or is he young?"

"Both. But his mother, if I'm thinking of the right one ..." She looked at the ceiling, thinking. "I'm not positive, but I think he'll be big. If I'm thinking of the right mama, she's huge."

Chevon looked at Katelynn for confirmation, which Katelynn did not give. Chevon looked at the woman. "Can I pick him up?"

"Don't see why not."

She scooped him up in her arms and knew. This was the one. She nuzzled her face into his cheek, and he purred loudly.

"He seems to like you."

"The feeling is mutual. Can I take him?"

"Of course. Do you like the looks of any others?"

Chevon laughed. "I do, but I better not. Thanks so much." She waited for the woman to say something more. When she didn't, she turned and headed toward the door, carrying her new cat who seemed content to let himself be lugged out of the house.

As soon as the girls got back into the car, Katelynn said, "No, really. You are such a weirdo."

Chevon laughed. "Maybe, but can we make one more stop?"

"I really can't. I have to get home."

"It will only take a second." Chevon didn't want to disrespect Katelynn's schedule, but she was nervous to go to Fanny's house alone.

Katelynn didn't argue.

Chevon sped toward the woman's house, her sense of urgency heightened by the kitten's caterwauling and Katelynn's constant sneezing.

"Did you know you were allergic to cats?" She tried to make the question light, tried to convince Katelynn she was having a grand time. It occurred to Chevon that she was acting crazy again.

"Yes." She sounded as if someone was physically pinching her nose shut.

Chevon pulled in front of Fanny's house and pulled the cat off Katelynn's shoulder. This proved harder than she'd thought it would be as his claws had quite a purchase on Katelynn's coat.

"Dude." Katelynn looked out her window. "Where are we?"

Chapter 30

Chevon

"You were right," Chevon said. "I am a total weirdo." She looked out Katelynn's window. "This is my friend's house, and I'm about to give her this cat."

Katelynn laughed heartily. "Does she *know* you're going to give her a cat?"

"No."

Still laughing, Katelynn said, "Wait. Does she know she's your friend?"

Chevon joined her in her laughing. "Sort of. Come on."

Katelynn shook her head, hesitated, but then climbed out of the car. "Is life with you always this exciting?"

She started to say no but then thought that yes, maybe it was. Lately, anyway. Her heart hammered so hard it hurt. Her legs were cold in more ways than one, but she forced them to Fanny's front door.

When she got there, she hesitated, not wanting to let go of the cat with one hand so she could knock.

Turned out she didn't need to. Fanny opened the front door, looked down at the cat, and cooed. "Well, who is this?"

Words didn't come, and Chevon swallowed hard. Part of her expected Katelynn to jump in and explain, but Katelynn did no such thing. She stood ten feet behind.

"Would you like to come in?" Fanny looked a bit baffled.

Chevon found her voice. "Sure." She stepped up into the house, and then they both waited for Katelynn to join them, which, after a few seconds of consideration, she did.

The warmth of the home jolted Chevon's tongue free. "Fanny, I'm sorry to say that I don't think Hissy Fit is coming back."

Fanny's eyes grew wide.

"We've hung signs all over town. I've even prayed about it"—Katelynn scowled, but Chevon didn't have the mental space to regret this admission—"and he's not back. So ..." She took a deep breath. "So I found this little guy, and he needs a home, and I thought maybe you two could help each other."

Fanny looked at the cat like a woman looking at a newborn baby. "He *is* some beautiful."

Chevon stretched out her arms toward Fanny. At first Fanny hesitated, but then the cat's back legs slipped out and dangled, bicycling in the air as they tried to find purchase somewhere. Fanny's arms shot out and scooped him up, drawing him into her chest. He nuzzled against her neck, home.

Chevon waited for her to say something. "So?"

Fanny looked at her.

"Do you want him?"

Fanny smiled. "Yes, dear. Thank you." She closed her eyes and sighed. "Hissy Fit."

Alarmed, Chevon said, "That's not Hissy Fit."

"I know, but it's such a good name."

That was a small relief. "But he needs a name of his own, don't you think?"

Fanny opened her eyes, looking thoughtful. "I don't know. What's another name as good as Hissy Fit?"

Chevon had no idea. "Uh ..."

"Bubblebutt," Katelynn said.

Chevon looked at her, bewildered.

Fanny laughed and held the cat out in front of her, looking into his eyes. "No, he doesn't look like a Bubblebutt. He needs something more ... distinguished."

Like Hissy Fit was distinguished?

"Something like King Henry, or no ... Sir Henry, but more catlike ..."

"Sir Pounce?" Katelynn offered. "No, Sir Pounci*ful*."

"Yes!" Fanny cried. "Sir Pounciful!" She looked into the cat's eyes again. "Do you like that? Sir Pounciful! That's perfect!" She drew him into her chest again and looked at Chevon with wet eyes. "Thank you so much, dear. I love him. I got to say, I was a little annoyed when you church people came to my door, but now I'm so happy."

Chevon forced a smile. "That's great. Well, my friend needs to get home, so you two take good care of each other." She hurried to the door.

As soon as they were outside, as Chevon had feared, Katelynn said, "*You* church people? You lied to me!"

Chevon sighed and hurried for the car. "I didn't lie. I go to church because Jason wants me to. Doesn't mean I buy into all the religious nonsense." She put her hand on the door handle and stopped.

Katelynn had stopped moving. "But you said you prayed about her cat."

"I did. I was desperate. And that was the only prayer I've ever prayed. Now, are you going to get in the car?"

Katelynn pivoted ninety degrees. "I'll walk."

"Katelynn, don't! That's silly! It'll take you fifteen minutes to walk from here!" Chevon stopped. She was still walking. Shoot. It was a good thing she wasn't one of those "church people" because she was really bad at it.

She got into the car and slammed the door, mad as a hornet. Stupid Katelynn. She'd felt so good after helping Fanny, and then Katelynn had to go and ruin it. She put the car in gear and glanced into her rearview mirror before pulling out and saw Katelynn running back toward her. Whoa.

She stepped on the brake, and Katelynn pulled her door open. "I'm sorry, can you give me a ride?" She was already in the seat.

"Of course. What's wrong?" She stepped on the accelerator.

"Just drive."

"I am! What's wrong?"

"My sister just called. My mom is freaking out."

"Why, because you're not there?"

She laughed bitterly. "You make it sound like my mom needs a logical reason to freak out."

"Katelynn," Chevon said softly, "what's wrong with your mom?"

"She's just ... not well. She's depressed. And she drinks a lot. But it's okay. It's okay. I'm managing."

Chevon turned onto her street and stepped on the gas. "I'm sorry."

"Thanks. But it's really okay."

Chevon pulled into her driveway and stopped.

Katelynn jumped out.

"Do you want me to come in?"

Katelynn laughed. "Uh, definitely not." She paused. "Thanks, Chevon. You won't tell anyone, right?"

Chevon nodded. "Right."

Chapter 31

Lauren

Lauren was supposed to meet Esther at the church, but she was running late. Victor had knocked a canning jar off the countertop and in fear of getting in trouble, had cleaned up the mess himself. Unfortunately, he'd done an insufficient job, and Judith had stepped in the glass with both feet. So there was blood all over the kitchen, and Judith was wailing, sure she was going to bleed to death.

By the time Lauren got the bleeding stopped and the glass and blood cleaned up, she was fifteen minutes behind. Then Peter needed help with his math.

"You know what? You've got the day off. No more math today." She opened the door.

"That's not fair!" Mary Sue cried. "He acts like a dummy, so he doesn't have to do anything?"

"Don't call your brother a dummy!" Lauren pulled the door shut behind her before she could hear anything that would make her stop. She looked toward the barn. "I'm leaving! Be right back!"

There was no answer.

"Did you hear me?"

Still nothing.

Frustrated, she stomped up the slight incline toward the barn. As soon as her husband was in sight, she said, "Did you hear me? I said I'm leaving."

He glanced up. "Okay."

He didn't seem to understand how this affected him. "Okay, so the kids are in the house."

He looked at her. "Yes, Lauren. I know we have children."

She tried not to glare at him. "I'll be right back."

"Good luck."

This annoyed her. He didn't wish her luck. He didn't want her doing what she was doing. She'd only gotten away with it because it had been Esther's idea.

Her annoyance hadn't faded when she got to the church to find four women waiting. Esther and Vicky were there, as expected, but so were Barbara and Tonya. "Uh ... I'm not sure we should show up with an army."

Vicky pursed her lips but didn't say anything.

Tonya looked at the others. "I don't have to go."

"I think you *should* go," Vicky said. "That's why I invited you. You didn't come to the tea," she said accusingly, "and we need her to know this church is more than a bunch of old broads."

Tonya looked at Lauren. "Isn't that what you have Lauren for?"

Vicky looked at Lauren. "Oh yeah." She hadn't thought of that. "Are you going, Lauren?"

"Of course she's going!" Esther said. "She's our connection to this woman."

Vicky gave Esther side eye. "Don't act like you've never delivered a pie without a connection."

Esther didn't argue.

Vicky looked at Barbara. "What about you? You don't need to go."

Barbara's mouth fell open. "I never get invited to anything! Why did you guys even invite me to start this church with you in the first place?" She grabbed her giant satchel and stormed toward the door.

"Hang on, Barbara," Tonya said. "Let's go have. I don't want to go back to work yet."

Barbara didn't reply, but she did slow down.

"There." Vicky looked at Esther and then back to Lauren. "Just the three of us."

Suddenly, Lauren wanted to get this over with. She looked at Esther. "Are you ready?"

"Yes. And the pie's getting cold."

"Let's go then."

"Are you driving?" Vicky asked without specifying whom she was asking. "I think Tonya just stole my car."

"She didn't *steal* it," Esther said. "I can drive, but my car's back at the apartment building."

"I can drive," Lauren said loudly. Why not? Her minivan only had two hundred thousand miles on it. What were a few more?

The closer they got to the house, the more nervous she grew. "What are we going to say, exactly?"

"Hi, Molly," Vicky said. "We made you a pie."

That didn't seem like a normal thing to say. "And you guys have done this before?"

"Been doing it since the seventies."

"Yes, Lauren," Esther said. "If you'd like, I can do the talking." She sounded none too eager.

The fact that she'd volunteered despite this lack of inclination touched Lauren. "I'd appreciate that."

And then they were there. Lauren started to pray but wasn't even sure what to ask for. Courage? Calmed nerves? The right words? Sanity? All of the above, she decided, as she slammed the door. *Just give me whatever I need, please.*

Esther and Vicky stood back and let Lauren do the knocking. Molly answered after the first knock. She didn't look surprised to see them. Despite the fact that Lauren had no intention of talking and no idea what to say, her mouth opened and spilled words. "You left kind of suddenly the other day, and we wanted to make sure you were okay. So we baked you a pie."

Molly looked down at the pie. She took a deep breath. "Look, I don't want to be rude, but I've given it a lot of thought, and I just don't think this church stuff is for me. Thank you, though, for your kindness." She started to shut the door.

"Don't you want your pie?" Lauren asked quickly, sounding a little too desperate.

"No, thank you. I'm gluten free."

As she shut the door, an image of her eating a gluteny tea-party cookie flashed through Lauren's mind. She turned toward the others. "Shoot."

Neither Vicky nor Esther looked surprised. Or even particularly disappointed.

Lauren stepped down off the step, and Esther lay the pie in the spot her feet had vacated.

"I don't think she wants the pie."

"We always leave the pie," Vicky said and turned toward the street.

Chapter 32

Chevon

In a moment of lovestruck weakness, Chevon had agreed to go to Thursday-morning Bible study with Jason. Now Thursday morning was here, and Chevon really regretted that promise. She didn't even want to go to school, let alone get up early for Bible study.

She groped around in the dark for her phone, found it, and then texted, "I don't feel good."

He didn't answer immediately. Was that because he wasn't awake yet? Or had she irritated him? She had been complaining about her stomach a lot lately. She texted again. "Like much sicker than usual." Was the word *sick* a lie? Maybe. She didn't feel nauseous at the moment. It was more like an overall malaise. A paralyzing lack of energy. She'd call it tired, but she couldn't sleep. She'd call it depressed, but there weren't many negative thoughts. She was just ... blah.

Still no answer.

Fine. "I'm going back to bed," she texted, even though she hadn't gotten out of bed yet.

She rolled onto her side, set the phone on the nightstand, shoved her hands under her pillow, and closed her eyes.

Her phone chirped. Seriously? She opened one eye to look at it, but no information was available from its current angle. It was obviously Jason. Who else was going to text her at five-thirty in the morning? She grabbed the phone and opened the text.

"You promised."

Wow, guilt much?

Another text appeared. "I think it will help."

Help who? Certainly not her. Help him? Did he really care what these people thought about him and his ability to get his pregnant girlfriend to a Bible study? Who even went to this thing, anyway? Hype and two eighth graders?

"We'll pray for you to get better."

This one annoyed her more than any text ever had. "You can pray for me without me there. Not going." She pressed send, slammed the phone down, and squeezed her eyes shut.

It chirped again, but she didn't take the bait.

Chapter 33

Esther

It was time for another boots-on-the-ground-for-Jesus Saturday. Esther had lost her motivation. She'd also lost track. How many Saturdays had this been? Three? Four? There were only supposed to be four, so she thought this could only be number three. Surely she'd have heard some celebratory scuttlebutt if this were their last hurrah.

"Do I really have to go again?" Zoe whined, her head in the fridge.

"Isn't Levi going?"

"I don't think so. I'm having trouble talking him into it."

"No." Esther sighed as she bent over to pull her boots on. "You don't have to go."

"Really?" Zoe's head popped up.

The joy on her face made Esther chuckle. "Really. I'm not going to force you to do this sort of thing."

And yet, Zoe was all bundled up and standing by the door when Esther reached it.

She raised an eyebrow. "Change your mind?"

"I don't want to make you go alone."

"I won't be alone." There were fifty other people involved in this circus. "I have Walter."

Zoe snickered. "Do you *want* me to skip it so you've got a better chance of being alone with *Walter*?"

Esther playfully swatted her arm. "Of course not."

They tromped through the snow toward the church. They'd gotten about four fresh inches the night before. Esther was glad Derek had been tucked in safely with Walter.

They stepped into the partially heated sanctuary, and Walter smiled at them. Derek stood beside him. She walked over to them. "Hi, Derek. Nice to see you. Thanks for joining us."

Derek didn't reply, but Walter bent to give her a peck on the cheek, which, despite all the previous pecks on her cheeks, still managed to make her blush. She scanned the room, taking a quick, silent roll call.

Zoe must have been doing the same thing because she said, "The Puddys aren't here yet."

"They've still got a few minutes." Except that a glance at the clock told Esther that they didn't. It was go time.

Pastor was already handing out assignments. He handed Walter a photocopied map.

"Richie's Head?" Walter immediately said.

Pastor stopped walking. "Yes. Is that a problem?"

Walter frowned. "*I* live on Richie's Head Road."

Pastor, his confusion apparently surpassing Walter's, backpedaled. "I don't understand."

Walter lowered his voice. "I don't think there are many people in need in that neighborhood."

Understanding spread across Pastor's face. "You mean that's where all the rich people live?"

Esther knew Walter well enough to know he wasn't going to like that comment, but he hid his annoyance well.

"I don't think there are any rich people in Carver Harbor, but yes, that's where the employed homeowners live."

The ones with million-dollar homes and multi-million-dollar views, Esther mentally added.

"People can be wealthy and still be poor in spirit," Pastor said.

Now Walter's annoyance was clear. "Again, we're not wealthy, and what is that supposed to mean?"

"It means"—What was going on? Was Pastor getting irritated too?—"that rich people have problems. They have heartbreak. They have broken marriages. They have heroin addictions—"

Walter interrupted with a derisive laugh. "I don't think there are any heroin addicts living on Richie's Head Road."

Derek sidestepped away from the two men, who had grown quite loud now.

Esther reached out and took the map. "Thank you, Pastor. We'll do our best to find someone to help."

Walter gave her a dirty look but waited till Pastor walked away to say, "This is going to be a complete waste of time."

Esther sighed. "Maybe. But we could say that about our last two Saturdays as well. Maybe we'll have an easy go of it. Maybe people won't cuss us out and slam their doors in our faces."

"Rich people are even ruder than poor people."

Esther noticed his use of the word *rich*, but she didn't say anything.

Derek had no such convictions. "See? Lots of rich people in Carver Harbor." He looked at Walter, his face deadpan. "Wealth is relative. So is addiction. There are addicts everywhere, in every town, on every street. And don't forget. *I* live on Richie's Head Road."

Chapter 34

Cathy

Cathy watched Chevon walk in, her eyes on the heels of Jason in front of her. He came to a stop, and she stopped beside him, but still she didn't look up, as if her head were too heavy for her to lift.

Cathy started toward her, dodged some small talk on her way across the room, and finally arrived at her side. "How are you feeling, honey?"

Finally, she looked up. Cathy found some relief in the fact that she was able to.

"I'm fine."

Cathy didn't buy that for a second.

"I talked to Katelynn."

Wow! She hadn't even thought to ask. She'd been too worried about Chevon. "That's so great!"

"Quite a bit, even. I've been giving her rides home."

Cathy couldn't remember being so thrilled. "Wow, Chevon. Good for you!"

Chevon gave her a cryptic look. "Good for me? I didn't do it for me. I did it for Katelynn."

Cathy nodded. "I know." Chevon didn't yet understand that helping Katelynn would be good for her too. "So is she okay?"

Chevon looked Cathy in the eye for several seconds. "Could we maybe go somewhere private?"

For the first time, Jason paid attention to their conversation.

"Of course. Right this way." She quickly led her to the office.

"Sorry," Chevon said as soon as they'd stepped into the small room. "I'm not trying to be dramatic, but Katelynn begged me not to tell anyone. In fact, there's not much to tell. Yes, her mother drinks, but it doesn't sound like it's that big a deal. It doesn't sound like they're neglected or abused or anything. Katelynn helps out with taking care of her siblings."

Chevon might not think this was a big deal, but it sounded like a nightmare. "Honey, that's a lot for any teenager."

"I know," Chevon said, her words clipped, "but it's better than the alternative."

"What's the alternative?"

"The stupid state getting involved and coming in and making things worse, taking Katelynn's brothers and sisters away from her."

"Oh, I don't think they'd do that," Cathy said even though she thought that might be exactly what would happen. "Who told you that would happen?"

Chevon pressed her lips into a straight line. "Look, I told you what I know, even though I told Katelynn I wouldn't tell anyone. And no one is in danger. So can we just let Katelynn take care of her family the way she has been and leave them alone?"

Cathy considered how to respond.

"And she knows I'm here if anything does go wrong. I've sort of been lumped in with you helpful church people now, whether I like it or not."

Cathy wasn't sure what she meant by this, but she liked the sounds of "you helpful church people." Were they getting a reputation, perchance?

"Is that all?" Chevon asked.

She was the one who'd invited Cathy in for the chat, but Cathy let it slide. The girl had a reason or two to be a bit snippy.

"You bet." She opened the door and held it for Chevon, who left in a hurry.

Cathy returned to her friends. "I know I said I'd go with you gals today, but I'm going to have to jump ship."

"What?" Barbara cried, indignant, as Rachel said, "Okeedoke."

"Thanks for understanding. You two will be fine on your own." She turned to find Chevon again and caught sight of her going out the door. She hurried to catch up. "Yoo-hoo!" she cried, trying to sound light and jovial but sounding instead too much like an old biddy. "Mind if I tag along?"

Chevon groaned. "Thought we were finally going to get to go without a *grownup*." The word carried a thick layer of irony.

Jason gave her a scolding look. "Of course. That's fine, Cathy."

Good, because she was going to climb into that car with or without permission.

Jason was still looking at her. "Would you like to drive? Your car is more reliable."

She smiled. That boy did not care one hoot about reliability. He cared about gas money. Or maybe he just wanted to ride in a car with a working heater. "Of course. Let's go. It should still be warm." This was a great development. Now she wouldn't have to talk someone else into stopping at Katelynn's house. She would just do it herself.

Chapter 35

Esther

As they drove out toward Richie's Head, Esther paid more attention than usual to the houses. Most of them had been there for years, and she'd gotten so used to them that she paid them no mind. They were simply part of the scenery. But now she wondered. *Were* they rich? Were they wealthy? How much money did they have? And an even more interesting question: *how* did they get that much money? Certainly not from Carver Harbor. All these people must be from away. She looked at the man driving the car. All but Walter, maybe?

"This seems to be the first house in our area." He sounded as though he were pulling into the dentist's parking lot.

Esther patted his hand. "It won't be so bad." Her go-get-'em attitude was as fake as plastic. She didn't want to be here either, but she felt guilty expressing that.

"You guys want me to do it?" Zoe started to get out of the car.

Unwilling to let the youngster show her up, Esther hustled to catch up, and Walter and Derek followed shortly thereafter.

Zoe got to the door first and knocked.

Someone answered quickly, before Walter could get there. The woman looked familiar, but that didn't mean much. Esther could have seen her in the grocery store. She smiled brightly. "Good morning! My name is Esther, and we're from New—"

"Walter!" the woman cried. "How are you?"

Esther's mouth snapped shut. Her first thought: Walter couldn't have mentioned that he knew these people? And right on the heels of that: of course he knew these people. They were his neighbors.

"Hi, Maddy. I'm well enough. How about you?"

"I'm good, I'm good. What brings you guys out in the cold like this?" She looked past them. "Car trouble?"

"No, ma'am. I'm a part of New Beginnings Church now, and we're going around town checking on folks, seeing if anyone needs any help with anything."

She furrowed her brow. "Help?"

Walter looked a little sheepish. "Yes. Help. With literally anything. I'm not promising we can answer every request, but we're just trying to make it known that we care. You know, reaching out."

She nodded, chewing her lip. "Well, as a matter of fact, Stan is inside resting." She stepped outside and pulled the door shut behind her. "He's not feeling so good. You know he's on the list for a liver donation."

Walter nodded stoically. "Yes, I'm sorry to hear that."

"Well, we sure would appreciate your prayer. If you guys would ask the others in your church to pray too, the more the merrier."

"Of course." Walter nodded.

"We could come in and pray for him right now," Derek said. "Lay hands on him and all that."

Her eyes flitted to Derek and then froze there. "No, thank you. Like I said, he's resting."

Walter nodded quickly, and the movement of his head seemed to pull her eyes away from Derek's face. "We will absolutely do that. Keep me posted, please? We'll all keep praying until we hear from you."

She let out a long breath, seeming relieved. "I'd sure appreciate that."

"It's the least we can do. Go back inside and get warmed up. Let us know if you need anything else."

She smiled. "Thanks, Walter." She glanced at Esther. "And everybody else." Then she turned and scuttled back inside.

Esther turned to see that Zoe was almost back to the car.

"Did you know he needed a liver?" Esther asked under her breath.

"No," Walter said. "One thing I've learned in my many trips around the sun. When people are in crisis, they always assume everyone else knows they're in crisis, but everybody else is too caught up in surviving their ordinary day-to-day to notice."

Esther didn't know what to say to that.

"I've suffered a few crises on my own." He sounded so sad.

She looked at him quickly, shocked at how profoundly the sadness in his tone affected her. Her chest ached, and she found it hard to breathe all of a sudden. This was a new Walter: a vulnerable, injured Walter. She was overwhelmed with the desire to comfort him, to care for him, to make sure no one ever injured him again. Trying to get her breath under control, she climbed into the car. "I'm sorry that you've ever suffered anything."

He gave her a small smile. "Thanks, honey. I love you."

She hadn't yet told Walter that she loved him, and she wasn't sure she wanted the first time to be in a car with Zoe and Derek, but she *was* sure of something else in that moment. She *did* love him, and she wanted to make darn sure he knew. "I love you too, Walter."

"Awww," Zoe said from the back. "You guys are adorable."

Walter chuckled and put the car in drive as Derek started singing "Jingle Bells."

Chapter 36

Esther

Walter had a bit of a spring in his step as he approached house number two.

"Do you know these folks too?" Esther hurried to keep up with his long strides.

"No, sure don't. I don't think they've lived here long. This house was for sale not long ago."

Esther looked up at the front of the house that spread out before her. She couldn't begin to estimate its square footage. "Whoever they are, they must have paid a pretty penny for this little cottage by the sea."

"Not as much as you'd think," Walter said. "Carver Harbor isn't exactly the Portland waterfront."

No. That was for sure. It was so much better.

Walter rapped on the door, and a pretty middle-aged woman answered. She offered a smile, but there was suspicion in her eyes. She looked Derek up and down as she said, "Can I help you?"

It occurred to Esther that if they were going to continue taking Derek on these little outings, they should buy him a new coat and hat. Or maybe they should do that anyway.

Walter launched into his spiel, and the woman's face lit up. "Honey!" she called over her shoulder before Walter had finished. "Come here!"

A man appeared behind her with an expectant look on his face.

"These people are from ..." She looked at Walter. "Sorry, I got so excited, what's the name again? New ..."

"New Beginnings."

She looked up at the man whom Esther presumed was her husband. "They're from New Beginnings Church, and they've stopped in to see if we need anything."

The man didn't recoil at the news, but he was certainly less excited than his wife. "New Beginnings. What a great name for a church."

Esther tried not to look too proud. "Thank you. We think so. God gives each of us a new beginning each day."

"Isn't that the truth!" The man leaned on his door frame, and Esther shuddered to think how much heat they were letting escape as they chatted. "What denomination?"

Walter's eyes jerked toward Esther.

"No denomination," she said. "Just Jesus."

The man's mouth spread into a smile. "I like that."

"Have you ever noticed the beginning of the word *denomination* sounds a lot like the word *demon*?" Derek asked.

Esther froze, desperately wanting him to stop talking with no idea how to make that happen.

The man gave Derek a quizzical look. "No, I hadn't noticed that."

"It does, though, doesn't it?" Derek continued. "Have you ever noticed that we name things in an attempt to control them?"

"Anyway!" Esther said loudly. "Welcome to Carver Harbor! Is there anything we can do to help you settle in?"

They both stared at Derek, speechless. Then, when Derek started whistling "Jingle Bells," the man's lips spread into a small smile. More amused now than bewildered.

"We were *just* now talking," the woman said with a little more volume than she'd used before, in order to be heard over the whistling. "I mean literally when you knocked on the door, we were talking about how we needed to find a new church. We've been dragging our feet since we moved. There's been so much to do, and we were so sad to leave our old church. It's hard to start over. Where are you located?"

Walter rattled off the address.

"Isn't that right up the street from the old folks' home?" she asked.

Esther bristled. "There's an apartment building there on the corner, yes."

"Terrific! What time is the service?"

"Ten-thirty."

"Great! We'll see you there!"

This was all going so smoothly, it seemed the four of them weren't sure how to react. "Great!" Walter finally said. "See you there."

She smiled again. "Thanks for stopping by. Gave us just the kick in the butt we needed." She stepped back and shut the door, and the four of them turned away.

"Wow," Zoe said. "These first two houses went so well, I think we should skip the third."

Esther laughed. "Not a chance, kiddo."

Zoe had been right. The third door was slammed in their faces, but it didn't dampen their spirits one bit. They carried their good news and their prayer request back to their church with a newfound energy.

They had made a difference today, and it felt amazing.

Chapter 37

Cathy

The teenage girl Cathy now knew was Katelynn ripped her front door open and glared down at Chevon. Cathy opened her mouth to defend the young woman beside her, but then couldn't find words when Katelynn stepped outside and slammed the door behind her. "Isn't it illegal to harass people?"

It was an empty threat, and the girl had to know it. No way this child was going to involve the law.

The girl looked past Cathy toward the two teenage boys still sitting in the car.

Cathy hoped they weren't staring. "Katelynn."

Katelynn's eyes jerked toward her. She hadn't been expecting to hear her name, apparently.

Cathy tried to sound gentle and loving, but her voice came out matter-of-fact. "We're not here to cause you trouble. I only wanted to introduce myself. My name is Cathy, and I care about you and your family. God has blessed me in many ways, and I want to praise him for that by trying to bless you. I am not an enemy. I am not here to interfere with your life in any way."

It appeared she was speechless. Her eyes flitted back and forth between Chevon and Cathy.

"You have a big family. Do you have enough food?"

Katelynn didn't answer.

"Could we bring you some groceries?"

Still no answer.

"Okay, we're going to bring you some food. What do your brothers and sisters like to eat?"

She shrugged. "Anything sweet."

Cathy smiled. "Good. Anything else?"

Her eyes darted around, avoiding eye contact. "They like cereal. Mac and cheese. Hot dogs ..."

Cathy waited for the list to continue, but it didn't, so she asked, "Are you warm enough? Do you have enough oil or wood?"

She didn't answer.

Cathy's stomach rolled. How were these kids managing? "Do you burn oil? Wood?"

"Oil," she said quietly.

"Great. We'll have some oil delivered. How about clothes? Do you have enough coats and boots?"

"Yes," she snapped. "The kids have clothes."

"Good, good. Can you think of anything else we can do?"

"What, are you guys rich or something?"

Cathy laughed. "Hardly. But like I said, God continues to bless us so that we can bless others. He has literally given us groceries so we can give them to you. We're like a storehouse. That's why we work so hard to find people to share with. We need to keep the blessings flowing through us." Cathy could tell she was losing her. She stepped closer. She wanted to reach out and take the girl's hand, but they were both shoved into her pockets. How could she make this girl feel her love? *Believe* in her love? "I've been around a while, Katelynn. I've seen some things. Nothing can surprise me or horrify me. If you need anything, you call me, okay? Or you call

Chevon. God loves you so much. He wants to take care of you and bless you."

She almost sneered, but she didn't argue.

"We get together every Sunday morning at ten-thirty. There are doughnuts, coffee, hot chocolate. There's music and love and most importantly, there's God. You are welcome to join us. I could even pick you up here and take—"

She laughed coldly. "I don't think so."

Cathy nodded. "That's okay. Just know that there are a whole bunch more people there wanting to love on you and your family." She sighed. "Let's just say you have family there you haven't met yet." She stepped back. "And you don't all have to go. Maybe just you want to go. Or maybe just a few of your siblings. Any combination, any time, but no pressure and no hurry. We'll be there when you're ready, and until then, you know how to get in touch with us." She smiled. "Go back inside and get warm. We'll get the food and oil here as soon as possible."

She nodded. "Thank you." She looked at Chevon. "Sorry I got mad." She was speaking so quietly Cathy could barely make out the words. "I'm actually pretty excited to be able to turn the heat up. I keep it pretty low."

Chapter 38

Erica

"Go back inside and get warm. We'll get the food and oil here as soon as possible."

Erica edged closer to the window, wanting to figure out who her daughter was outside talking to, but not wanting to be seen.

Katelynn was talking, but Erica couldn't make out a single word.

"Mommy, you're bleeding."

"Shhh!" She strained to hear Katelynn's words.

"Mommy!" He got louder, scared. "You're bleeding!"

"No, I'm not!" she snapped. "Now be quiet!"

The voices outside stopped, and she froze. Had they heard her?

He whimpered. "Yes, you are." He was definitely scared, but he didn't need to be. Katelynn had stopped the bleeding over an hour ago. She'd cleaned up the mysterious wound, stopped the bleeding, and then bandaged it.

Katelynn turned to come back inside, and Erica backed away from the window. As she did so, she saw the fear in her son's eyes and reached for him. "I'm okay, honey. I'm okay. I'm not bleeding anymore." She peppered his face with kisses.

"You are bleeding," Katelynn said, looking down at her leg. She sighed. "Have a seat. I'll change your bandage."

Erica looked down to see blood trickling out from beneath the gauze and tape. Her stomach churned. What on earth had she done? She'd already searched the house for evidence of the accident, something sharp with blood on it, something at calf level, but she hadn't found anything. Had she left the house last night? And if so, where had she gone? She needed to ask Katelynn, but she really didn't want to. She needed a drink. Then she'd be able to ask Katelynn.

"Hang on, honey. I need to get a drink. Then you can fix this."

"You can't wait two minutes? Let me fix it and then you can get a drink."

Erica looked at her daughter, surprised. Katelynn's tone was downright sassy. Her daughter never sassed her.

"No, I can't. Just give me a minute."

Katelynn rolled her eyes and sat on the coffee table.

Erica poured some vodka into some V8, gulped it down, and instantly felt better. Her stomach's complaints were cut in half, and her head cleared within seconds. Her leg still hurt, but she deserved that. She returned to the couch and sat down in front of her daughter, who took her leg into her kind, gentle hands.

"Honey," she began and then was overwhelmed with love for her daughter. What an amazing young woman this girl was. What a kind soul. "Do you know if I left the house last night?"

Without looking up she shook her head. "I don't think so, but I did sleep some." The voice was still irreverent, though her hands were patient and gentle.

"Who were those people?"

Katelynn sighed and looked up. "I told you. The church people. They keep coming around."

She hadn't told her anything about church people. A burning panic bubbled in her chest like acid. "What do you mean, church people? What church people? What do they want?"

She hesitated. "For the third time, they want to help. They're bringing us groceries, sending us ..." She stopped.

"Sending us what?" she pressed.

"Nothing. You have to hold still so the scab doesn't pull away from the cut. Can you just lie down for a few hours? Then I think you'll be okay."

"I don't need to lie down."

"No, Mom, you don't. What you *needed*, what I *told* you that you needed was to go get stitches, but since you refused, will you please lie down and rest, so I don't have to keep doing this?"

Erica slapped her daughter's hand away. "You know what? I didn't ask for your help, and I don't need it!" She probably *had* asked for her daughter's help, though, hadn't she?

Katelynn gave her a sad look. "Fine. Do it yourself. And when it starts bleeding again, don't come crying to me." She stood.

Erica's eyes burned. She reached for her hand, tried to pull her back. "Katie, I'm sorry. You know I'm not feeling well. Mornings really aren't my thing."

She yanked her hand away. "Yeah. I know."

Erica watched her daughter stomp off. There had been something she wanted to say, but what was it? Katelynn had said or done something that scared her, and she'd needed to ask about it, but now she couldn't remember what it was.

Chapter 39

Lauren

It had been so much work getting her family to church on time that Lauren wondered if it had been worth it. Maybe they should just take the winter off. As it was, Peter was wearing mismatched boots, and Victor hadn't brushed his teeth. He'd sworn he had; she'd known he was lying, but she'd waved a white flag in the name of getting everyone into the minivan.

Now she was grumpy and sitting in a hard wooden pew.

"Doughnut?" her husband asked.

She usually didn't partake, but she nodded. "Sounds great. The chocolatier the better." She watched him walk away and noticed there were a lot of visitors today. Had Pastor's little experiment actually brought people through the door? She sighed. Surely hadn't worked for Molly.

"Good morning!"

She turned front to see Esther leaning on the pew in front of her.

"Morning, Esther." She stood to embrace her.

"It's so good to see you. I was a little worried about you yesterday."

Lauren reeled back. "We miss one workday, and you panic?"

Esther's face fell, and guilt stabbed at Lauren's chest.

"No, no, I didn't mean that at all." She forced a laugh, which sounded nervous. "I just worry about everyone all the time. It's in my nature."

Lauren didn't believe this to be true. She took a deep breath. "I'm sorry, Esther. I didn't mean to snap. I just couldn't manage it yesterday. We are so far behind on chores and school. I could barely get everybody here today. I've just been ... a little ..." What was the word she needed? Every one that popped into her head was sinful. Discouraged? How dare she? Overwhelmed? Give it to God, then! Frustrated? Stop trying to control things! Let go and let God!

Esther squeezed her arm. "It's okay to be tired, Lauren," she said softly. "You are running a farm, and you have a hundred children."

Lauren laughed. "Thanks, Esther."

Roderick returned with two doughnuts. The powdered sugar on his lips suggested he'd already had one on his way back. He exchanged pleasantries with Esther, and then she winked at Lauren. "Try to relax and enjoy the service. And if you nod off, Pastor will live."

Lauren chuckled.

Roderick looked at her expectantly. "Why did she think you might nod off? Did you tell her we think Pastor's preaching is boring?"

Lauren sighed. "No. I didn't tell her that. I'm just tired, and she can tell."

They both sat down, and he looked at her thoughtfully. "Maybe you need a vacation."

She raised an eyebrow and chuckled sardonically. "Yeah, like that would be possible."

He pushed the doughnut into her hand. "Why not? I'm pretty sure I can keep the kids alive for one week. Maybe you could fly somewhere warm. Maybe you could go with your sister?"

Her heart warmed at the thought. She did miss her sister. "Maybe," she said, but as soon as she said it, she dismissed it. She couldn't leave her life right now, not even for a week. She didn't want to miss that much time with the kids, and besides, she needed to be around if Molly called.

With his mouth full of doughnut, Roderick pointed his chin at a couple Lauren hadn't seen before. "Who are they?"

Lauren shrugged. "No idea. But they look really well-dressed for Carver Harbor."

Zoe, who'd been sitting in the pew in front of them looking down at her phone, turned around. "They're new to town. They live on Richie's Head. We invited them to church yesterday while we were making our rounds."

"Oh, wow!" Roderick exclaimed. "That's fantastic!"

It was fantastic, and Lauren knew she should be excited. So why was she sad instead?

Chapter 40

Chevon

Chevon gasped.

Jason looked at her quickly. "What? What is it?" He glanced down at her stomach but then followed her eyes to the door.

"Fanny. Fanny just walked in."

"Who's Fanny?"

Chevon sighed. How quickly he forgot things that mattered to her. "The cat lady."

"Oh!" Jason's sincere excitement almost made up for his absentmindedness. "Are you going to go say hi?"

She kind of wanted to but she was feeling shy all of a sudden. "I don't know, should I? Is that a thing?"

He laughed. "Yes, that's a thing. When you invite someone to church, you then go welcome them when they show up."

She narrowed her eyes. "I don't know these things, Jason. I'm new at this game." Not to mention it was a game she didn't even want to be playing. Though right this second she was having quite a bit of fun. But she wasn't going to tell him that. "Never mind. Cathy's on it."

"You should still go," he said gently. "You guys have bonded." He hesitated. "You want me to go with you?"

"No." She stood up. She could go greet an old woman without help from her boyfriend. "You stay here." Stepping over and around legs, she extricated herself from the pew and headed toward Fanny.

"Hello, dear!" Fanny exclaimed when she saw her. "Don't you look pretty!"

This bewildered her a little. She wasn't dressed up or anything. Then she realized Fanny had never seen her without a winter coat on. "Thank you." The shyness was creeping in again. "How is Sir Pounciful?"

Fanny's face lit up. "Oh, he's magnificent! I hated to leave him, but I had to come see you and tell you how happy he is! He won't leave my side, constantly snuggling and purring up a storm. I just love him to pieces!"

Cathy's eyes grew wider as Fanny talked, and Chevon was quite proud of herself. See? Take that, church lady. She'd done a good thing!

From the front, the pastor asked everyone to sit.

"Would you like to sit with me?" Chevon asked, a little stunned at the brightness of her voice. She sounded a little like pre-pregnancy Chevon.

"That would be lovely!" Fanny adjusted her purse strap, smiled at Cathy, and then stepped toward Chevon.

"Right this way!" Again, the joy in her voice puzzled her.

And the look her boyfriend gave her when she returned with Fanny on her heels made her laugh out loud. "Jason, you remember Fanny. Fanny, this is my boyfriend, Jason."

Fanny held out a hand. "Handsome devil, you are!"

Jason accepted her handshake as his cheeks reddened. Chevon found this incredibly satisfying. It took a lot to make Jason DeGrave blush.

"Do you have Hissy Fit's picture, by chance?"

Chevon groaned. How could she keep forgetting to return that? "No, sorry. I will get it back to you. I've been really forgetful late—"

Fanny held up a hand. "Don't worry about it. Keep it. I've got plenty of others."

"Welcome! Welcome!" the pastor cried with his hands out. His excitement was a little extra. He needed to calm down. "It is so good to see so many familiar faces as well as some new ones. Welcome to New Beginnings! Rachel is going to lead us in some singing, so let's lift our voices to the Lord! And don't worry if your voice doesn't sound good to your own ears. It will sound great to God!" He stepped aside, and Rachel took his place.

The first song was an upbeat number, and though Chevon didn't particularly enjoy ancient church songs, her toe started tapping. She never sang along, didn't know any of the tunes to any of these songs, but she felt a bit of pressure to at least fake it, now that she had invited a friend to church. So she started lip-syncing.

Halfway through the second verse, she saw Jason looking down at her, and he appeared to be beaming with pride. Her lips froze. The satisfaction on his face annoyed the snot out of her. *No, Jason, you haven't won me over. No, you haven't turned me into a religious nut like you. I'm only doing this for Fanny, and I'm not even really singing.*

He looked confused, maybe even injured, and then turned his eyes back to his hymnal. She felt a little guilty for glaring at him but brushed it aside and focused on her lip-syncing.

This was no easy task, as these crusty old songs were *complicated.* That's one reason Chevon hated them. They were full of hard, weird words strung together in impossible ways that made no sense. If she ever were to try to sing along, she was sure she wouldn't be able to. Half the time it sounded like they were singing lines from some awful Shakespeare play. And even if she could manage singing the right words, she would have no idea what she was saying. Did any of these people understand what they were singing about? Cathy, maybe. Jason? Probably not.

The second song started with a long intro, and Chevon's toe stopped tapping. Bummer. Another dirge. She was about to lose focus when a line with crystal clear meaning jumped out at her. It was such plain English that it startled her. These people had just sung, loudly and proudly, the most juvenile words. The order was still Shakespeareish, but the words were not. She looked around to see if anyone else was reacting, but nope, it seemed to be business as usual. People seemed to be in some sort of trance, singing at the ceiling. Even though they'd just sung that God had devoted his sacred head *for such a worm as I.*

A *worm*? What on earth? Did some second-grade boy write that? She wasn't a worm! None of these people were worms! What an absolutely strange thing to sing! Several seconds after the fact, she laughed aloud. Jason gave her a quizzical look, and she pointed at the word in his hymnal as she mouthed, "*Worm?*"

He read the word, smiled, and muttered, "I'll explain later."

All amusement left her. She was so tired of him acting like the old wise religious man training the idiot who didn't know anything. She didn't need him to explain anything. She knew what a worm was. Hot with annoyance, she returned to her lip-syncing. "My God, why would you shed your blood, so pure and undefiled, to make a sinful one like me your chosen, precious child?" The words hit her without warning. She grabbed the pew in front her to steady herself as her throat swelled with emotion. She understood those words too. Her legs gave out, and she plopped down into the pew.

Jason dropped beside her and put his arm around her. "Are you okay? What's wrong?"

She shook him off. "Let me go. I just need ..." She didn't know what she needed. "I just need to breathe."

"Is it the baby?"

"Let me go!" she snapped loudly—too loudly. She looked around to see if anyone was looking, and countless people were. She caught Cathy's eye and immediately looked down at her lap.

At least Jason had let go of her. She pulled herself to her feet. She had to get out of there. "Excuse me," she said to Fanny, and then went as fast as she could to the bathroom.

With fumbling hands she locked the door behind her and then leaned on the sink. She caught sight of herself in the mirror. Her face was rounder than it had been a week ago, and her eyes filled with tears. This was all too much. She hated this so much. Maybe she should have known being a pregnant teen would be this much of a roller coaster, but she hadn't. She turned on the water, splashed some onto her face, and then wiped it off with a paper towel.

She stood up straight and looked in the mirror. There. That felt a little better. She was okay. Just a rush of hormones, probably. Yet the words kept scrolling through her mind: Why would you shed your pure blood to make a sinful one like me your chosen child? She sucked in some more air as she stared at herself. "Are you sinful?" she whispered to the reflection. She didn't think so. She'd never done anything bad. Sure, she was an unwed pregnant teen, but she'd never hurt anyone. And yet, that song had said she was a worm. But she wasn't, was she? She wasn't a worm. Or was she? Maybe she was a worm in comparison to how pure God was. Her brain couldn't really make sense of that idea, but her gut understood it perfectly.

She stood there, trying to get her mind to catch up with what her gut knew: God was pure. She wasn't.

Could it be that simple?

And despite this, he wanted her to be his child. Somehow, she knew this too. Not because Jason had told her. If anything, his telling her over and over had worked against her knowing. She didn't want him to be right about something that she was wrong about. And not because Cathy had told her either. Or Vicky. Or Esther.

She knew it because she knew it. She didn't know how. She just knew it. God was perfect. And he wanted her to be his child. Even though she was a worm. She laughed aloud and immediately felt better. Then she felt like a complete lunatic for standing in the church bathroom talking to her reflection and then laughing. She wiped her face again and looked in the mirror. "Okay, God," she said aloud. "Help me get through the rest of this service. I don't need to be acting like a pregnant lunatic on a roller coaster in front of other people." She laughed again, shook her head as she threw the paper towel into the trash bin, and then left the bathroom.

When she got back to her pew, Jason leaned over and kissed her on the cheek. "You felt him, didn't you?" he said, and his voice was so gentle that she nearly melted into a puddle.

Still, she wouldn't give him the satisfaction. "Just a bit queasy is all."

He tickled her side. "Not true, and you know it. He's real. I told you so."

Jason didn't know when to quit. She didn't answer him, but in her head, she said, *If you're real, God, you'd better prove it to me.*

Chapter 41

Cathy

Cathy spent most of the service praying for Chevon. She'd witnessed her having some sort of spiritual moment, she was sure of it, but she couldn't tell what had happened. She'd considered following her to the bathroom, but she knew that would be too pushy. And so she'd just prayed that Chevon would feel God's presence, that she would feel his love, and that he would reveal himself to her in a way that she couldn't talk herself out of.

That kid was one tough cookie. Cathy really liked her. She was confident and had her head on straight. It delighted Cathy to think of all God could do through her. But first, he had to go after her heart.

Pastor gave a rousing altar call that was so persuasive, Cathy knew it had come straight from God. A few people went down front, but Cathy didn't know them. She sneaked a look at Chevon, who was watching them pray at the altar. Her expression was sober, but Cathy couldn't read more than that. It occurred to her that she could offer to go to the altar with her, but a still, small voice told her again not to be pushy.

She took a deep breath and pulled her eyes away from the girl. *Yes, Father. Thank you. I'll try to be patient.* This made her think of Katelynn. Why wasn't she having more success with that family?

They'd dropped off two boxes of groceries the day before, and no one would even answer the door. Why had all these other people had so much more success getting their people through the doors? What was she doing wrong?

The still, small voice whispered, "*Patience*," and she had to smile. Ah, yes, there it was again. She'd never been good at it, and so God kept giving her opportunities to get better. She took a long breath. Maybe if she got better at it, he wouldn't make her wait so much.

She closed her eyes and focused on the music, which Fiona so miraculously played. What a blessing that woman was! She didn't talk much, or ever, really, but she showed up week after week and delivered music more beautiful than any Cathy had ever heard. The woman had once made albums. Now she played for New Beginnings. And yet, she seemed content, enjoying every note. Thank God for her.

The service ended, and without trying to orchestrate it, Cathy's path crossed Chevon's. "Hi, honey. How are you feeling?"

"Fine. Katelynn texted me last night. She said thanks for the groceries. Apparently her brothers were really excited about the Fruity Pebbles."

Cathy's heart leapt. "Oh, good! Well, as you see her this week, keep your ears open for anything else they need."

Chevon nodded. "Already on it. I like Katelynn. She can be a little rude sometimes, but I can't blame her as I sort of forced myself on her after years of not talking to her." She took a breath. "Anyway, I've got some room in my life now for some new friends." She glanced at Jason, who'd kept walking. "I used to hang out with Jason's ex and her friends, and well, needless to say, they're not really into me anymore."

Cathy chuckled. "You may one day look back on that and see it as a gift."

Chevon nodded, and her expression was older than her years. "I already do." She looked around the room. "Besides, now I have all this." She smiled. "I have all of you."

"That you do. Whether you want us or not." Cathy gave her hand a squeeze, and the women shared a genuine, synergistic laugh. And Cathy thought that, patience or no patience, the authentic joy of that laugh would sustain her for some time.

Chapter 42

Lauren

Lauren felt better after church, and her afternoon passed in a blissful symphony of family chaos. But now that it was dark and quiet, she couldn't force her mind to rest. She prayed for calm, asked for a quiet mind, but peace didn't come. Instead, her fretting picked up in intensity until around midnight, when she couldn't bear to lie there anymore.

She sat up. *I'll just go to the kitchen, find a snack*, she thought. She just needed to get out of that room, move around a bit. But once she was in the kitchen, she knew her fretting had evolved into something else, something much more powerful: raw fear.

She was terrified.

She tried to slow her breathing, tried to be reasonable. Why was she so scared all of a sudden?

Molly. She was scared for Molly.

She was scared because Molly was scared.

This jump seemed like a reach even to her, and yet she couldn't dismiss it. She glanced at the door, at her coat hanging beside it. She couldn't just go to Molly's house and pound on the door at midnight. The woman already thought she was a freak show. She turned away from the door. No. Calm down, she told herself.

She feared she was verging on a bona fide panic attack, and she didn't know what else to do, so she went and knelt in front of her couch and began to pray. But the praying didn't make her feel any better.

The fear kept increasing.

She needed help.

She went back to her bedroom and, fully knowing he would be upset with her and needing him anyway, shook her husband's shoulder.

He blinked away the sleepiness and then stared at her. "What?" he whispered, not unkindly.

As she searched for words, he sat up and turned on the lamp. He rubbed her arm gently. "What is it, honey? What's wrong?"

She pushed the words out, and they came out squeaky, so far from her own voice she might have laughed if she wasn't so terrified. "I think something's wrong with Molly."

She expected him to scoff, but he didn't. He only studied her. His hand slid down to hold hers and then he looked down at it. "Goodness, your heart is pounding." He lifted his eyes. "So what do you want to do?"

"I don't know," she whimpered. And it was true. She had never been a woman short of ideas. She was always full of them. Many of them were often silly, impossible, or downright terrible, but she still had them. But now there was nothing.

He nodded and pulled the covers back. "Let me up. I'll go tell Mary Sue she's in charge."

She got out of his way. It took several seconds for the meaning of his words to register. He was going to wake up their oldest daughter. So they were leaving the house. She hurriedly threw on jeans, a bra, and a sweatshirt, and then she followed him up the stairs to Mary Sue's room.

"No," she heard him say. "You don't even have to do anything. I just wanted you to be aware that we're leaving. We'll lock all the doors, so you'll be locked in."

Lauren stepped into the doorway.

"And you can call if you need us." He leaned over and kissed Mary Sue on the forehead.

"But why can't you tell me where you're going?"

"It's just grownup stuff. But I promise you, nothing to worry about. We're going to help someone, but there's nothing wrong with your parents." He turned toward Lauren. "Come on, let's go."

She followed him back down the stairs, surprised at his pace, surprised he wasn't arguing with her, reasoning with her, surprised at all of this.

The truck seat was so cold it hurt. "I'm sorry about all this. I don't know ..." She didn't know how to finish that sentence.

"Let's hope this is all nothing, and you can apologize then." He turned the key, and the heater blew cold air at her. She shivered. "For now, you have nothing to be sorry for." He backed out of the driveway.

"What's the plan?"

"Don't have one. I'm currently praying for one. Right now, I'm just going to drive toward Molly's house. Then I don't know what."

Lauren started praying too, and hot tears rolled down her cheeks, cooling by the time they reached her chin.

"This might be a stupid question, but you don't have her phone number, correct?"

"No, I don't. And I don't know anyone who does."

"That's what I was afraid of. Okay. I'm wondering if we should call the police now. It's going to take forever for them to get here. The closest they might be is Bucksport. How sure are you that we're going to need them?"

"I'm not sure of anything."

He chuckled dryly. "Okay. Let's not call them yet."

They were quiet the rest of the way to Molly's street, and Lauren prayed as hard as she could. A new fear for her husband had been layered over her old fear for Molly.

The house came into view, and Roderick swore softly under his breath. All the lights were on. He stopped on the street, rolled down the windows, and killed the engine. He closed his eyes, and Lauren held her breath.

Shouting.

He jumped out of the truck. "Call the cops." He headed for the front door, and Lauren followed, her cold fingers fumbling with her phone.

The operator answered as Roderick pounded on the front door. Lauren gave the address and then said, "Please send police. There's domestic violence here, and I think it's pretty bad."

Police and paramedics were on their way. Next door a porch light flicked on, and a woman stepped outside in a nightgown. "What's going on?"

Lauren didn't know how to answer that, so she didn't.

More shouting, a cry, and the sound of breaking glass.

"Open this door, or I will break it down!"

Was her husband even capable of breaking down a front door? As he backed up, she realized she was about to find out. He lowered his shoulder and drove his body into the door. It made a cracking sound, but it didn't give way. She prayed. Should she stop him?

What should she do but stand here stupidly ten feet behind him? The operator asked her if she was still outside the house.

"Yes."

"Don't go inside. Wait for the police."

Lauren didn't argue. Roderick threw his body into the door again.

A woman screamed—a loud, desperate, quavering scream. Roderick grabbed a snow shovel, jumped off the front steps, ran to the front window, and swung the shovel like a baseball bat. Glass exploded, the woman next door shrieked, and Roderick grabbed the windowsill and pulled himself inside, efficiently if not gracefully. Lauren ran, slowly through the snow, her boots not cooperating with her pace, to the window.

"I'm calling the police!" the woman in the bathrobe cried accusingly.

Yes, please do.

Molly lay on the floor, her arm resting over her bloody face. Roderick had already pulled Trevor away from her and was dragging him toward the door. Wanting to climb inside to help Molly and unsure if she'd be able to, Lauren grabbed the windowsill. A shard of glass stabbed at the base of her thumb and instinctively she yanked her hand away. Molly whimpered, and Lauren was going to try again when the front door clicked open.

Back through the snow Lauren tromped. She was watching her feet, so she didn't see her husband throw the man off the steps into the snow, but she heard him land. Then she was free of the snow and running up the steps.

She ran to Molly and knelt by her side. "Hey, Molly. Help is on the way. Hang in there." She looked her over, looking for some wound to tend to, something to clean, something to fix—but she was helpless, useless.

Molly opened her eyes, one of which was nearly swollen shut, and looked at her. "You," she said. "You did this."

Chapter 43

Katelynn

Katelynn woke up to the sound of her mother vomiting. She opened one eye and looked at the clock. Her alarm would have gone off in five minutes anyway. Not as bad as usual.

She swung her legs out of bed, slid her feet into some old sneakers to protect them from the cold floor, and headed for the bathroom. The door was locked, but she couldn't hear any more vomiting. Shoot. Had her mother passed out in there again? She knocked softly so she wouldn't wake her brothers and sisters. "Mom? I need to pee."

"Just a second," came the muffled reply.

Good. Not sleeping on the bathroom floor. Katelynn hated peeing in the backyard, especially in the winter.

The door slid open, and her mother came out wiping at her mouth. She looked down at Katelynn's feet. Really? Katelynn could understand her being embarrassed the first and second time this happened, maybe even the third, but the hundredth?

"You okay?"

She nodded and shuffled toward her bedroom. "Yeah, just ate somethin' that didn't agree with me. You know how sensitive my stomach is."

Yes, she sure did. She went into the bathroom, slid the window open, and then held her breath as she took care of business as fast as possible. She left the window open and shut the door to keep the cold from invading the rest of the house, reminding herself she *had* to shut that window before she left for school. She'd forgotten once or twice before.

She went to the kitchen and started a pot of coffee. Then she went to her bedroom to find something resembling clean clothes to put on. She hadn't been to the laundromat in over a week. She needed to make time to do that, but it was hard to time it right for when her mother was able to drive her. For the millionth time, she wished she could take driver's ed like everyone else in her class, but the price made that a pipe dream. She needed to get a job, which was fairly feasible in the summer months, but she didn't like leaving her brothers and sisters home that long without any supervision.

With her clothes on and her hair in a messy bun, she returned to pour a cup of coffee. Then she reached for the whiskey bottle in the cupboard—but it was empty. She rolled her eyes. Why had she put an empty bottle back into the cupboard? She rummaged around looking for another bottle, and finally found one with a few inches of whiskey left in it. She poured a shot into the coffee and then carried the mug to her mother's room.

She gave a perfunctory knock on the door and then went in and set the mug on the nightstand. "Mom? Your coffee."

She rolled over. "Oh, thanks, honey. That will help."

"I know." She went back to the kitchen to pour herself a cup and then sat down and closed her eyes. She was going to have to wake the kids up soon. She ran through the day she had in front of her. History paper due. It wasn't done. She might be able to pass off her first draft as a final. Math test. She wasn't ready for it, but she only needed a seventy to keep her grade above failing, and that was all that mattered. Just get the credits so she could get out of high school. She heard her mother coming and opened her eyes.

"Shouldn't the kids be up?"

"I'll get them in a minute." Katelynn looked out the window. "Did you hear those sirens last night?"

"Yes," she said quickly. Too quickly.

They had woken Katelynn up. They'd scared her. Her first thought was that they were coming for her mother. She'd lain there and listened to them until she was sure they weren't getting louder, and then she'd fallen back to sleep. "I wonder what it was about. Not many sirens in Carver Harbor."

"Probably just an ambulance."

"Maybe. But there was more than one of them."

"Probably that Cooper kid then. He's always in trouble. One of these days they're going to put him away for good."

Katelynn smirked. Her mother had hated Kendall Cooper since Little League. Her smirk slid away. How hard it was to believe now that her mother had ever been a Little League mother.

Chapter 44

Lauren

Lauren hadn't gotten to bed until well after sunrise. By the time she woke up three hours later, Mary Sue had already gotten her siblings fed, mostly dressed, and started on their school.

Lauren went to her, gave her a bear hug, kissed her on the cheek, and said, "You are so amazing. I love you."

Mary Sue squiggled out of her grasp. "That's your one hug for the day, Mom."

Lauren laughed. "How'd you like to do a little more babysitting today?"

Mary Sue groaned and gave her an are-you-serious look, but Lauren knew she mostly didn't mind. Mary Sue liked to be in charge.

"That woman we helped last night, she's in the hospital now. I'd like to go visit her. It won't take long."

Mary Sue's face grew serious. "Do I know her?"

Lauren measured out her coffee grounds and dumped them into the pot. "Not really. We met her at one of the houses we stopped at."

"Yeah, I thought so. I figured it was the woman you've been worried about. I prayed for her too. Is she going to be okay?"

"Yes," Lauren said, finally feeling confident about that. "Yes, she is."

"Sure, I'll babysit."

"Thanks, honey." She went to hug her again, but Mary Sue dodged her.

"Uh-uh. You've already met your limit."

Lauren laughed and went into the living room to call Esther. She told her the whole story and then asked if she'd like to go to the hospital with her.

Esther agreed and suggested they also invite Vicky.

Lauren wasn't so sure about this, but she was too tired to argue. So she hung up, took a lightning-fast shower, got dressed, and then returned to a full pot of coffee. She poured some into a coffee mug and then it occurred to her that she hadn't yet seen her husband. "Where's Dad?"

"He had to go get grain."

"Oh. Did he seem okay?"

Mary Sue looked up suspiciously. "Yes. Why, did you guys fight?"

"No, no," she said quickly. "He just didn't get much sleep either." And she was wondering if the police's suspicious, incessant questioning had taken a mental toll. They'd had trouble believing he'd needed to break a window.

Even though he had.

The neighbor's testimony had ended up helping. She'd said she'd heard multiple screams, then seen the crazy man smash through the front window, and seconds later throw the man outside.

This had satisfied the police.

"Be good for your sister," Lauren told the other children. "Finish your spelling and your history, and then you can take the rest of the day off."

Mary Sue was visibly relieved.

"Really?" Victor chirped. "On a Monday?"

"Yes, on a Monday. But only if you're good for your sister." She looked at Mary Sue. "I'm locking you in. Stay inside until one of us gets home."

"I know, Mom."

"Bye. Love you all to the moon and back a zillion times." She backed outside, closing the door behind her, and breathed in the fresh air. It had warmed up considerably since she'd gone to bed.

She picked up Esther and Vicky at the church and then drove to the hospital. The roads were treacherous with ice, but it didn't squash her spirits. After days and days of worrying about Molly, the woman was finally safe, and Lauren could finally have some peace. She knew that Molly would now begin a new set of struggles, but she also knew she and the others would walk with her through them.

She wasn't nervous until she got to Molly's door. Was the woman still mad at her? She tried to tell herself it didn't matter. She'd still done the right thing, whether Molly knew it or not.

Esther carried a bouquet of flowers. Nothing fancy. It had only come from the small Carver Harbor grocery, but still, Lauren was glad she'd brought it.

She took a deep breath, knocked on the door, and then opened it. She peeked inside, and immediately Molly's eyes met hers. "Can we come in?"

"Sure."

That was a good sign. Lauren stepped inside with the others right beside her.

Vicky gasped. "Oh dear!"

Lauren gave her a dirty look. "Don't listen to her, Molly. You're already looking a lot better." And she was. The swelling had gone down a lot.

"I wish I felt better."

Lauren crept closer and saw the cast on her arm. "I bet you do. Is your arm broken?"

She nodded. "My wrist."

Lauren's shoulders sagged. "I'm sorry."

"It's okay."

She didn't seem mad anymore. Lauren walked around to the far side of the bed to give the others more room. She walked by a half-eaten piece of gluteny toast and suppressed a smirk.

"Is there anyone you'd like us to call?" Lauren asked. "Any friends or family?"

"Someone needs to call Trevor's mother."

That wasn't what Lauren had in mind.

"I don't know if she knows he's in jail."

"I can do that," Vicky said. "How about someone for you?"

She looked down at her good hand. "Nah. I'm all set."

Vicky stepped closer. "I thank God you are okay. In time, you will realize that's who saved your life last night. God."

It was hard to read Molly's expression, but Lauren didn't think that Vicky's words were settling well.

"But I want you to know," she continued, "that as long as I'm able, I am here to help you." She glanced up at Esther and Lauren. "And that goes for the others too. They've got kids to attend to, of course, but they'll still make time for you." She looked back to

Molly. "So between all of us, you'll have someone to call on when you need it."

"Why?" Molly said, her voice raspy. She looked right at Lauren. "Why on earth do you guys care so much?"

"Because God," Vicky said before Lauren could answer. "Here. I wrote down some phone numbers for you." She set them on the table beside the gluteny toast. Then she pulled a chair away from the wall and started to sit.

"I'm a little tired," Molly said quickly. "I'd think I'd like to take a nap."

Vicky stood back up, seeming unsurprised. "I understand. We'll come back later to check in on you."

Lauren studied Molly's face, but she couldn't tell if this was received as good news or bad. "Have a good nap, Molly. I'm glad you're okay."

Molly gave her a small smile. "Thank you." Her words were heavy with meaning, more than a reflex. They warmed Lauren's soul.

Lauren patted her leg and then followed the others out of the room. When the door had shut behind them, she asked, "Are you really going to call that guy's mother?"

Vicky sneered. "Of course not. Don't be ridiculous. Let him rot."

Lauren bit back a grin. Amazing how Vicky could go from super-Christian to mean old hag in a second's time. "We need to be on guard, though. These men usually come back."

Esther looked at her. "Walter said he's in pretty deep. He resisted arrest, pulled a knife and assaulted one of the officers."

Lauren's heart lurched. Thank God he hadn't pulled a knife on Roderick. It occurred to her that Roderick hadn't given him a chance, and her chest swelled with pride.

"Walter told me what his bail would probably be. I don't remember the number, but it sounded impossibly high."

"Good." Vicky held the door open for them. "Like I said, let him *rot*."

Chapter 45

Chevon

Chevon caught Katelynn on the way to the art room. "Hey!" She gently bumped into her.

"Oh. Hey."

Chevon wished she were a little happier to see her. "Can I ask you something?"

"You're going to anyway."

Chevon laughed, though she didn't know if Katelynn was joking. "Why do you eat in the art room?"

"Because I would rather starve than eat in the cafeteria."

"But why?"

She stopped walking and looked at her. "Are you really going to make me say it? I don't have any friends, okay? I'm a total loser, and my art teacher is my only friend."

"You have a friend, Katelynn."

Katelynn didn't look excited about that. She started walking again, and Chevon fell back into step. "How did that start, anyway, you eating in the art room?"

She shrugged. "I asked if I could work on my art during lunch, and then it just sort of happened. Mrs. Movack knows what my life is like."

"She does?" Chevon asked, her words asking more than one question.

Katelynn stopped at the art room door, put her hand on the handle, and looked at Chevon. "Sort of. Not everything."

"Come sit with us today." Chevon was certain she'd say no, but she had to issue the invitation. She was surprised to realize that she also really *wanted* Katelynn to join them.

"With who?"

"Me, Zoe, Jason, Hype, Levi."

She raised an eyebrow. "Quite a combination you've got there."

Chevon swung her head toward the cafeteria. "Come on."

"Okay. Let me just tell Mrs. Movack that I won't be in today." She opened the door.

"Is this a trick?"

"What?"

"Are you going to go in there and leave me standing here until lunch is over?"

Katelynn laughed. "No. If I don't come out in sixty seconds, something's wrong, and come rescue me."

"Okay. Fair." Chevon waited, trying to pretend she wasn't conspicuous standing there in the middle of nowhere as the hallway emptied out.

Katelynn was back in seconds. "Lead the way."

"What'd she say?"

"She acted like she was excited for me, but I think she's also grateful to be able to eat alone."

"I doubt that," Chevon said, though she didn't know. She'd never taken an art class and had no idea how Mrs. Movack felt about Katelynn—or anyone else for that matter.

She felt Katelynn stiffen when they entered the din of the cafeteria, and she picked up speed. She bumped her hip into Hype. "Slide over."

Hype looked up, surprised. "Oh, hey, Katelynn."

Chevon was so grateful to him she could've kissed him. She looked at Jason, willing him to be as welcoming.

"Hey, Katelynn," Zoe said through a mouth full of food.

Jason didn't say anything, but he also didn't act annoyed that Katelynn was there.

"Hey," Katelynn said sheepishly. She sat down and tentatively opened her lunch bag. Their little table was full.

"Got anything good?" Hype said. "School lunch sucks."

Katelynn didn't say anything. She pulled out a small, prepackaged bag of baby carrots. Chevon recognized the brand from the church stash. "Ignore him, Katelynn. If you feed him, he'll never stop asking."

"Well, isn't this something, Jason?"

Chevon recognized the voice, so she didn't have to look up. Alita was hovering over Jason's head.

"I'm so glad you finally got what you wanted. To spend your time with the pregnant junior, the drunk"—she glanced at Zoe—"and the drunk lady's kid"—her eyes rested on Katelynn, who stopped chewing.

"Cut it out, Alita," Hype said.

"Or what, Hype? And why are you sitting with these freaks? Is social suicide trending right now?"

Jason stood abruptly, and Chevon finally looked up. He spun to face her. "Enough, Alita. You're embarrassing yourself."

She gasped. "Me? I'm the one embarrassing myself? Are you kidding me?" Her voice grew louder as she talked, and several tables nearby hushed their talking and stared.

"Yes, Alita," he said through gritted teeth. "Stop acting like you're better than anyone. Because you're not. You're not even good at anything except following makeup tutorials and blowing your parents' money."

Alita was so mad she started shaking. She glared up at Jason for several seconds before turning away. "Come on," she said to her friend who had already started backing away. "I don't have time for this."

Chapter 46

Lauren

Lauren nearly dropped the phone in surprise when she heard Molly's voice on the other end. She was being discharged from the hospital, and she needed a ride.

"Of course! I'll be right there."

"I think it'll be a few hours yet."

"Okay, well I won't hurry then. But I'll head that way."

Molly thanked her, and Lauren hung up. For about three seconds, she was floating on the clouds, but then a horrific thought knocked her to the ground.

Where was Molly going to go? She had no front window. She called Cathy. "Molly is ready to go home, and I just realized, her house has no front window! Do you have any ideas? I could invite her to stay here, but I don't think she'd be comfortable. It's more crowded than Grand Central. Can you think of anyone else who might take her in?" She was hoping *Cathy* would take her in. She thought Vicky probably had room, but she didn't know how much Vicky Molly could take.

"Let me make some calls. I'll call you back."

She called back in fifteen minutes. "Kyle's going to put in a new window today, and Joe's going to pay for it."

"Who?"

"Kyle. Barbara's son. You know, he's like an all-purpose handyman. He's done some work at the church."

"No, I know Kyle. Who's Joe?"

"Joe Weir. His family just started coming. He's from Bucksport."

"Oh!" She tried to picture him. "The one who's got older teens with him?"

"Yes. Though I think they might even be in their twenties. I'm not sure how old they are."

"He's going to pay for it? Wow, that's pretty amazing. Wait, wasn't he at that first Saturday workday?"

"Yes. First and second. I called Pastor, who called him to ask, and he said sure." Cathy said all of this without emotion. Did she dislike this newcomer? Lauren dismissed the thought. Cathy didn't dislike anyone.

"Wow, thanks so much, Cathy." She hung up and focused on getting herself to the hospital. She considered inviting another woman to go along, but it occurred to her she might keep seeking reinforcements because she didn't want to deal with these hard moments herself.

Maybe she should be relying on God instead of calling Esther every time she had an opportunity to serve someone.

When she said goodbye to Roderick, he offered to go with her. She declined, for the same reason she hadn't called Esther, but when his face fell, she reconsidered. "I want her to be comfortable talking to me, and I'm not sure she will if there's a man in the car."

"Good thinking." He chewed his lower lip. "Can I at least meet you there? I'd like to patch up that window, make sure her heat will keep up."

Lauren explained the new plan.

"Who's Joe Weir?"

She laughed. "I had the same question." She explained who he was, but the pieces didn't click into place as quickly as they had for her. "Never mind. He's a new member of the church. I'm sure you'll meet him soon. But yes, I'd love to meet you there. Might be good if you looked the place over and then tell her she's safe." She kissed him on the lips. "It's a good problem, you know?"

"What?" He scowled.

"We've got so many new people at church, new people helping even, that we no longer know everyone."

"Oh." He nodded. "New people is good. But I think it's always good to know everyone."

She nodded too. "True story. I'll text you when we're fifteen minutes out?"

He shook his head. "I'm going to talk to Mary Sue and then I'll go help Kyle. I'll be there when you get there."

"Oh good. Maybe you'll get to know Joe sooner rather than later."

He didn't look convinced. "Maybe."

She had to quit jabbering or she was never going to leave so she forced her feet toward the van. She waved to Peter who was peeking out the window, and then she was backing out of her driveway.

Her nerves increased as she grew closer to the hospital, but when she saw Molly, most of them dissolved away. "Wow, you look so much better!"

Half of Molly's mouth smiled. "The power of drugs."

Lauren couldn't think of any drugs that healed bruises. "I wouldn't be so quick to give the meds the credit. I think you're a strong woman."

Molly looked at her quickly, obviously surprised at her words.

"Stronger than you know."

She sat down to put on her shoes. "I guess we're about to find out."

Lauren didn't know what to say to that.

Molly stood up. "I don't know how I'm going to live now. I know Trevor wasn't perfect, but he was all I had. I don't have a job, and my headaches would make it hard to find and keep one. Besides, I don't know how to do anything anyway. So I don't have any money. The house is in his name. When he stops paying on it, I won't have that either."

Lauren stepped closer. "I have some experience with this. Not personally," she quickly added, "but I've been close to this type of situation before, and I promise, there's a way. We might not be able to see clearly right now, but thousands of strong women have gone before you, and they've been okay. I'll help. My church will help. More importantly, God will help."

Chapter 47

Lauren

When Lauren and Molly arrived at her house, the window had just been delivered. Joe Weir was nowhere in sight, and Kyle seemed happy to have Roderick's help. It wasn't a small window.

When Roderick saw the women approaching, he dropped his tools and headed toward Molly's front door. Then he waited there. He gave Lauren a sad look and then opened the door for them, motioning for them to go in first.

Molly whimpered when she saw the place. Somehow—maybe it was the daylight—the place looked worse than Lauren remembered it. There was broken glass everywhere, not only from the window but also from a lamp. There was blood on the couch, blood on the carpet, a smear on the wall.

Lauren shuddered thinking about what Molly had gone through here. Maybe she didn't *want* to stay here.

"She's not going to be able to stay here."

Lauren looked at him quickly, not following. Was he thinking what she was thinking? If so, that would be unusual, unprecedented even. Roderick didn't lack emotional intelligence, necessarily, but he wasn't exactly an empath.

"It's too cold. I dumped a few gallons of oil into the tank and bled the lines. We'll get it fired up as soon as the window's fixed, but it's still going to take hours to heat this place up." He took a deep breath.

He wasn't thinking about her emotional health. He was trying to keep her warm. Lauren's heart surged with affection for this man, for his sensible smarts.

"And some pipes froze."

Molly turned her eyes on him, and they weren't kind.

He hurried to say, "Kyle and I will fix them, but it will take some time."

"Maybe you didn't need to smash my living room window."

Roderick nodded, seeming unsurprised by this. "I'm sorry it came to that."

"He *did* need to smash your window, Molly. Seconds mattered. You could've died."

Molly looked away, toward the smear on the wall. "I'm not dead."

Lauren was bewildered. "You're not dead because he smashed your window!"

Roderick put a calming hand on her arm. "It's all right, Lauren. Molly, we'll get things fixed up good as new." He looked at Lauren. "In the meantime, I'm not sure where to take her. I don't know if the church has the heat on today."

Molly looked at her. "What, you can break into my house in the middle of the night, but you can't invite me to yours?"

"Do you even know why we were here at midnight?" Lauren asked.

The anger slid off her face. No, she hadn't thought of that.

"We were coming to check on you, Molly. We left our warm, safe house to come check on you because you were in *danger*. You were living in *danger*. And yes, you are welcome to come to my house right now. I have five children in twelve hundred square feet. I've got one bathroom, and sometimes the toilet doesn't flush. Oh, and when our goats get sick, they live in the house too. Would you like to come stay with us for a while?"

It appeared Molly had lost all her anger.

"Honey," Roderick said softly. Then he looked at Molly. "Of course you can come to my home, but I think we can find you a more comfortable spot." He returned his eyes to Lauren. "Why don't you start with the church? Call Pastor. If the heat's turned up today, that's as comfortable a place as any." Then more quietly, "And if the heat's turned down, it will still be more comfortable than this."

Lauren took a deep breath. "I'm sorry I got snippy. I am severely overtired. Does that sound okay with you?"

She nodded. "I wish I knew where my sister lived."

"Maybe we can do some online sleuthing, figure it out. But first, do you want to pack a bag? Maybe grab enough to spend the night somewhere?"

She nodded again and then whispered, "Be right back." She headed toward a hallway on the other end of the house, and she gave the blood spot on the carpet a wide berth.

"I called Vicky too," Roderick said quietly. "She and Tonya are going to come after school and clean this place up. Hopefully we can move her back in tomorrow." He shook his head. "I feel so stupid for not thinking of these things earlier."

She gave her husband a long hug. "You were doing a million other things. You're a good man, husband." She loosened her grip and looked up at him. "And you did need to smash that window."

"I know," he said, but he didn't sound happy about it.

Chapter 48

Esther

Esther hurried to meet Lauren and Molly at the church. Lauren had said that she'd already called Pastor and he would unlock the place, but it was unclear if he would physically be there when they arrived. Esther thought someone should be. She wanted the place to feel as welcoming as possible, and she was afraid they were going to beat her there. Lauren hadn't given her much warning that they were coming.

She stepped out of her building to see the church door swing shut. Had that been Pastor or Lauren and Molly? Her eyes swung to the street to find both vehicles. Everyone was there but her. She hurried down the walkway and then up the street, arriving at the church door out of breath.

Feeling a bit foolish, she tried to get a grip before swinging the door open. Oh good, she could hear the furnace running. Pastor had already turned up the heat. This was an act of faith in itself. Despite Walter's sizable tithes, they were still having trouble keeping that oil tank full. And the church wasn't even that massive. She wondered how those huge churches managed. She glanced up at the sky-high ceiling. That probably wasn't helping matters much. Not exactly an efficient design. What had those nineteenth-century folks been thinking? Didn't they go to church in the winter?

"Molly, you remember Esther?"

Molly turned to look at her, and Esther's heart ached for her. Her face was yellow with bruises, and her lips red with scabs. Molly nodded.

"Welcome back, Molly. Make yourself at home." Esther looked around. "Where did Pastor go?"

"He went to find her something to eat."

Esther scowled. "As in out of a box?" She shook her head. "I'd better go help him." She found him in the basement, staring at their well-stocked shelves.

"I was just down here," he said as she approached, "and I swear this is a totally different batch of stuff. Nothing even looks familiar."

"It is different. We have a pretty rapid turnover."

He looked surprised.

"What, did you think we just hoarded the same stockpile?"

He looked insulted. "I wouldn't use the word *hoarded*, but I didn't realize we gave away a mountain of food every week."

"We do. So what were you looking for?"

"Not sure. Something for her to snack on. But all I can find are these prepackaged cupcakes and that just didn't feel good enough."

The man had good instincts. "Why don't you go do pastoral things, and I'll whip her up something to eat?"

"As in cook it?"

Esther laughed. "Heat it up, at least. Won't take but a minute."

He looked relieved and turned for the stairs.

She followed him up them, though he gained a huge lead. She caught up eventually and asked Molly what sounded good.

She shrugged.

"Do you like spaghetti? I could heat up some garlic bread to go with it?"

She shook her head. "Spaghetti's okay, but no bread. It hurts too much to chew."

Of course it did. "Okay, I can do spaghetti. Or how about beef stew?"

A new expression flickered across her face. Esther couldn't quite read it. "Yeah, actually. That sounds pretty good."

"Beef stew coming up." She hurried back downstairs.

Once she got the canned soup into the pot and added her own seasonings, discontent wandered into her head space. She knew she was right where she was supposed to be, where she was good at being, and yet she longed to be upstairs getting to know the woman too. She looked in the fridge for something to drink and found some ginger ale. Wow, that was unexpected. And she couldn't remember any ginger ale coming in with any deliveries either. No one ever gave them soda. Was this Rachel's personal stash? If so, Rachel was about to share. She grabbed a ginger ale and headed up the stairs.

She handed the bottle to Molly, who thanked her politely. "Your stew is just about ready."

"Thank you," she said again.

Lauren and Pastor were still there, sitting near her, but it appeared they weren't doing much talking. Not wanting to join in the awkwardness, she turned to go back downstairs. Maybe she shouldn't have longed for the upstairs action. The grass wasn't always greener.

"Esther," Pastor called before she'd reached the stairs.

She turned back.

"Molly is going to spend the night at Rachel's house, so if you were worried about finding bedding, you don't need to."

Oh, what a good idea. "Sounds great." She smiled at Molly. "You're going to love Rachel. She's a real hoot."

Chapter 49

Esther

"This is the last Saturday, right?" Zoe said.

Esther wasn't going to let on to her granddaughter, but she was just as relieved as Zoe was. "For now, yes."

"I think we should keep doing it, but not *every* Saturday. Good grief."

"I know, but look at all God has done."

Zoe looked dubious.

"Zoe, think about it. Mr. Puddy probably saved someone's life. Cathy and Chevon are bonding with that family. We've fed people, kept them warm, prayed for them, and we have new people coming to church. This is the stuff of miracles!"

"Yeah. I guess when you list it all together like that."

"So, come on. Put some pep in your step!"

Zoe rolled her eyes.

Esther wasn't offended as she was faking her own pep. She fully believed in what they were doing, but she couldn't believe how exhausting it was. She thought of missionaries then. How did they keep up, day in and day out? She needed to up her prayer game for those missionaries.

As soon as they got to the church, Zoe made a beeline for Levi, who was standing beside his mom. Esther scanned the room, found Rachel, and headed that way.

"Nice hat."

Rachel beamed. "You like it?"

"I don't think I've seen that one."

"Just bought it."

What? How? There was a store still selling hats like that?

Rachel read her mind. "eBay."

"Ah," Esther said. She'd never spent much time on eBay. Though her daughter Christy had bought her a yarn surprise grab bag from the site a while back, and that had been delightful. Maybe she should do some shopping there herself. "How is Molly?"

"Good. The Puddys got her moved back in yesterday."

"How did she seem when she was staying with you?"

"Pretty quiet. I think she's got a lot of pent-up anger. For good reason, of course. I'm not judging. But she sure didn't want to hear about Jesus."

"That's okay," Esther said thoughtfully. "We have time, I hope."

"She's worried about her husband."

"I was afraid that might be the case."

"We'll have to keep an eye on her."

"Have we sent any groceries over?"

"Lauren took a few bags."

"Good. Well, I'm going to make her a real meal and take it over soon."

"Better you than me." They both laughed.

"Yes. Let's not further traumatize her."

Pastor stopped in front of them with a map outstretched. "Are you guys working together today?"

"No." Esther looked toward the door. "Walter should be here soon."

"And I'm waiting on Barbara."

"Okay, then. Here are two maps."

"Haven't we covered the whole town yet?" Rachel asked.

"Not even close," he said as he walked away.

Rachel let out a long sigh. "So many souls."

"That's okay. That's why there's more than one church to reach them."

Lauren came bouncing over, looking more like herself after a few weeks of not. "Rachel! Molly really likes you!"

Rachel grinned.

"Of course she does. Everyone likes Rachel."

"Not everyone," Rachel corrected firmly.

Esther laughed. "Close enough."

"No really. She likes you, so we've got to keep you two in touch. I've tried to be her friend. Vicky's tried. But she seems to have taken a liking to you."

"I believe she likes all of us. She's just not going to admit it in front of us. She said plenty of positive things about you and Vicky while she was at my house."

Lauren's mouth fell open. "Really?"

"Really. Well, more so you than Vicky."

Esther snickered, and then felt guilty. "None of us would be where we are right now without Vicky."

"She certainly has her strengths," Rachel said. "I'll give her that. Hey, where's Cathy?"

"She's not feeling well."

"Really?" Rachel said. "She never gets sick."

"I know, but it's that time of year."

"Okay, everybody!" Pastor called from the center of the room. "Thanks for being here. I know that some of this has been hard." He let out a long sigh. Was he getting choked up? "I got a call this morning from Natalie's son. The kids and I met her that first Saturday. She was a faith-filled woman fighting cancer. Her son asked if we could do her funeral here on Thursday. I said that we would be honored." He took a deep breath. "I knew this would be hard, and it's even harder than I thought it would be. I know in some ways it feels like we're not accomplishing much, but then something miraculous happens and I realize that God is working. He won't always do what we want him to or expect him to, but he's still working. And he certainly doesn't work on our schedule." He chuckled.

"So I'm asking you for one more day, two more hours of keeping the faith. One thing is for sure. God's Word does not return void, and that's what we've been doing these past weeks is acting out God's Word. So it won't return void. None of this is wasted effort. And even when we can't see the evidence, God is still working. He is working in this town, and he is working on the hearts of this town. So let's go do this last round with confidence in that fact! And then I'll leave you alone for a few weeks!"

Chapter 50

Erica

Katelynn sat on the other end of the couch and propped her feet up. She looked at the television. "Can I change this?"

Erica had no idea what she was watching. "Sure. Go ahead." She glanced at the clock. "It's after noon."

Katelynn stopped flipping through the channels and looked at her curiously. "So? Did you have somewhere to be?"

Erica snickered. No, she sure didn't.

Her daughter looked over at her pants. "Although now that you mention it, you are looking pretty put together. What's going on, Mom?"

Erica couldn't quite read her tone. Was that suspicion? Or only curiosity? She shrugged. "I don't know. I just like these pants." This was true. She liked them so much that she saved them for leaving the house, which she rarely did anymore. She couldn't remember the last time she'd gone somewhere other than the gas station.

Katelynn continued to stare at her. She wasn't buying it.

"Fine. I was expecting the church people. I thought I'd answer the door for once."

"Why?" Katelynn said quickly. "Why would you answer the door?"

"So they don't think I'm a horrible mother!"

Katelynn opened her mouth but then clamped it shut again.

"What? Do you have something to say?"

She shook her head and looked at the television. "No, Mom."

"You know I don't feel well. I have issues they can't even imagine."

"I know, Mom."

"So, anyway. I wasn't going to invite them in or anything. I was just going to show them that I have good days."

Katelynn finally looked at her. "That's actually a pretty good idea."

Now it was Erica's turn to be suspicious. "Why do you say that?"

Katelynn shrugged. "No reason. Just like you said, show them that you're a good mom. That we're safe with you. That they can stop worrying and leave us alone."

"Worrying? Are they worried about us?"

Katelynn tipped her head back and closed her eyes. "Ah, I shouldn't have said it like that. No, I don't think they're worried, but it would also be good to avoid that worry."

This made sense. "Oh." This was the longest, most normal conversation she'd had with Katelynn in weeks. She wanted to keep it going. "What *is* their deal anyway?"

Katelynn puffed out her cheeks and exhaled slowly. "They want to help people, that's all."

They watched TV for a few minutes as Erica tried to think of something else to say.

"Maybe we could go to a church service some Sunday."

Erica laughed. "What?" She waited for Katelynn to join her in her laughter. "Are you joking?"

"Nope." Her eyes were glued to the screen, but it seemed she was holding her breath.

"Why would you want to do that?"

She shrugged. "They're growing on me. Chevon is like an actual friend now. She's even got me in with the cool kids. I don't have to eat lunch in the art room anymore."

"You've been eating lunch in the art room?"

Katelynn rolled her eyes. "I've told you that like ten times."

She didn't think this could possibly be true. Her memory wasn't perfect, but it wasn't that bad.

Katelynn looked at her. "I have friends now, Mom. All because church people came and knocked on our door." She chuckled. "I can't believe it's true, but it is. And I like that Cathy lady too."

Erica didn't know who Cathy was. "Isn't Chevon the one who's pregnant?"

Katelynn nodded. "Yeppers."

This wasn't good. Katelynn shouldn't be around people who were bad influences. "And who are these other friends of yours?"

Katelynn looked at her incredulous. "You can't seriously be judging my friends?"

"I don't know yet! Who are they?"

"Jason, Hype, Levi, and the new girl, Zoe."

That didn't sound so bad. "And they're the popular kids."

Katelynn laughed. "Definitely not. I didn't say the popular kids. I said the cool kids. Though I guess Jason and Hype used to be popular until Jason decided he didn't want to be anymore." She sighed and ran a hand through her hair. "Never mind all that. The point is, I think it would be a good thing if we went to church. Just to visit. See what it's like. I've seen them. They don't dress up or anything." She looked at her mother's pants again. "Those jeans are perfect."

Erica couldn't think of a single thing she'd want to do *less* than go to a church service in Carver Harbor. She'd rather go to rehab. "Well you can go. But I'm not."

Katelynn gave her a sharp look. "No, I *can't* go without you, Mom, because I can't leave the kids here."

"What? Why?"

Katelynn hesitated. "Are you really going to make me say it?"

Erica wasn't sure what Katelynn was going to say, but she was pretty sure she didn't want to hear it.

After another minute of only the television talking, Katelynn said, "You know, they give people free stuff."

"Huh?"

"They give you free stuff. When you go to church there. They even give people money."

Something stabbed into Erica's chest and twisted. It took her breath away. Her whole body got hot, and she suddenly desperately needed a drink. She'd been trying to wait until after the church people left, but the wait was over. She got up and hurried to the kitchen. She ripped a glass out of the cupboard and filled it—half vodka, half fake cranberry juice—and took a long drink. Then she set the glass down and stared at the wall in front of her. Her whole body shook.

Had what she thought just happened actually happened? Had her daughter tried to blatantly manipulate her with the promise of free money? Who did Katelynn think she was? Some money-grubbing beggar? Did Katelynn really think she was that desperate? And not only desperate, but stupid? She saw that Katelynn was leaving the living room and hollered, "Hey!"

Katelynn turned around slowly. "I don't want to fight with you right now."

Erica took her glass and walked slowly toward her. "How stupid do you think I am?"

Katelynn scowled. "What?"

"How stupid," she repeated deliberately and slowly, "do think I am?"

"Mom, I don't know what you're talking about. I don't think you're stupid."

"Oh really? And yet, when you decide to try to manipulate me into doing something you want me to do, you don't even try to get tricky? You just say, 'Hey, Mom, you should do this thing because they'll give you free money!'"

Katelynn's eyes grew big. "They *do* give people free money! I wasn't making that up!"

"No, they don't!" Erica screamed. "That's the stupidest thing I've ever heard, but your lying isn't even the worst part! It's that you think I'm so pathetic that I would just run into a church building for free money. Is that really what you think of me?"

Katelynn started backing up. "Mom, listen. I have literally no idea why you're so upset, but I'm done talking about it. Forget it. I don't want to go to church with you. I obviously can't take you anywhere in public, ever."

Erica watched her go and then collapsed on the couch. She drained her drink and then she started to cry. She didn't even know what, precisely, those tears were for, but tears had never felt so necessary.

Chapter 51

Chevon

Chevon asked Jason to swing by Katelynn's house on their way to Sunday service. As they approached the house, she saw Cathy getting out of her car. She laughed aloud.

"What?" Jason asked.

"There's Cathy. Great minds think alike."

Jason pulled the car over. "So I guess you don't need me for this?"

"Aw, how sweet." She leaned over and kissed him on the cheek. "You can come too if you want."

He gave her side-eye. "Nah, I'll stay here and hold down the fort."

"Well, you are my knight in shining armor, so that makes sense." She climbed out of the car.

"Yeah, right," Jason muttered.

"Hey!" Chevon called, only a little embarrassed at how excited she was to see Cathy.

She stopped walking and turned to look. "Oh, hey! Great minds think alike, huh?"

"Ha! That's what I just said to Jason!"

Cathy stood still until Chevon caught up and then started for the door again. "We should send Derek over to shovel for these people. This is so treacherous."

"Or we could make Jason and Hype do it."

It didn't help that Cathy's boots had three-inch heels, but Chevon wasn't going to say anything about that. "I texted Katelynn already, but she didn't answer me, so I thought I would just pound on her door. She might not be up yet." Chevon didn't think this was true, but it gave Katelynn an excuse to ignore her text.

Cathy knocked politely before Chevon could get a chance to pound.

A little boy answered the door, and Katelynn came running up behind them. "Oh, hey, guys. I should have expected you." She stepped outside and pulled the door shut behind her.

"Wanted to see if you wanted a ride to church," Chevon said.

Katelynn looked at Cathy. "And you're giving her a ride too?"

Cathy chuckled. "No, I have my own car. But I had the same thought."

Katelynn's eyes went back and forth between them. "Sure, why not? Give me a second to get dressed." She went back inside and started to shut the door in their faces, but Cathy didn't let her.

Both surprised and amused by Cathy's boldness, Chevon followed her inside. The living room they stepped into was cluttered and dimly lit. The shades were drawn on every window, and only one lamp by the couch was lit. The TV was on, providing a little more light to the room.

A woman came down the hallway, saw them, and stopped in her tracks. "Katelynn?" she cried.

"Just a second!" came the faint response from down the hall.

The woman gave them a bewildered look and then turned and headed toward Katelynn's voice. "Who are those people, and why are they in my house?"

Chevon had to strain to hear Katelynn's words and resisted the urge to creep closer. "... and Chevon ... I told you ..."

"That's Chevon?" her mom cried. "She doesn't even look pregnant!"

Chevon's cheeks got hot, and Cathy reached over and squeezed her hand.

The little boy who'd answered the door looked up at her. "You're pregnant?"

Oh boy. She nodded.

"Can I touch it?"

She really didn't want this child touching her belly and wished she'd had the foresight to zip her coat up. But she also didn't want to disappoint him. "Sure."

He reached a tentative hand up and lay it on her stomach. "Whoa," he said.

"I forbid this!" the woman screamed, taking Chevon's focus away from the hand on her stomach. "I already told you that I forbid it!"

Chevon gave Cathy a worried look, but the woman looked surprisingly calm.

The boy dropped his hand and ran away. He hadn't even flinched when his mother had screamed—as if she was background noise.

Katelynn's mother swore loudly, and Katelynn came down the hall carrying a coat. "I'm ready."

Her mother caught up to her and grabbed her shoulder. "Please, Katie!" She was sobbing.

Chevon looked to Cathy for direction, but Cathy only stood there, still calm.

The woman fell to the floor, and Katelynn turned to look at her as if having second thoughts.

"Please, Katie. Don't go. I can't. I ... can't."

Chevon was overwhelmed with embarrassment for Katelynn. She was so glad Jason hadn't come in.

"Mom, I'm going to church. Deal with it." She started to walk past Cathy, and Cathy softly put her hand on Katelynn's arm.

"Hang on just a sec, honey." She looked past Katelynn. "Ma'am, is there anything we can do to help you?"

The woman sobbed harder. Tears and snot poured out of her as her head tipped forward toward the floor. "Oh, for God's sake, just get out."

Cathy didn't move. Chevon tried hard, but she couldn't read her. Why wasn't she leaving?

"Ma'am? We love Katelynn, but she's your daughter. If you are honestly forbidding her from going, then we're certainly not going to take her out of your home."

What?

"What?" Katelynn cried. "Then I'll walk!"

Cathy gave her a sad look. "That will be between you and your mother, but I'm not going to be a part of dishonoring your mother's authority here."

Katelynn shook Cathy's hand off in disgust. "You're ridiculous." She threw her coat. "Get out then."

Cathy looked at the woman on the floor. "It's up to you, ma'am. Do we have your permission to take your daughter to church?"

The woman didn't look up, and her stringy hair fell around her face, obscuring it. "Leave her here," she growled.

"Okay then." Cathy looked at Katelynn, who was throwing fire with her eyes. "Sorry, Katelynn. Maybe next time."

"Yeah. Or maybe not."

Chevon didn't know what to do. This was insane on every level. "Sorry, Katelynn. Text me later?"

She didn't answer, and Chevon followed Cathy outside. "What was that about?"

Cathy stopped walking and looked at her. "We cannot become that woman's enemy. We cannot come between her and her daughter." She glanced at Chevon's stomach. "I promise you. You'll understand very soon." She sounded so sad that Chevon was barely irritated with her know-it-all explanation.

Chapter 52

Erica

"I could not possibly hate you more!" Katelynn screamed.

Erica's youngest ran by her, scared of his sister's wrath. She tried to grab him, but she was too slow. She tried to get up, fell, and then tried again and managed. "I have to go get dressed."

Katelynn laughed, and it sounded sinister. "Oh, you do? Why do you have to get dressed, Mom? Why on earth do you have to get dressed?"

Shoot. She needed a drink before she could get dressed. She looked toward the kitchen, but her daughter—her daughter who had been rock-steady her whole life and had only recently lost her mind—stood between her and it. No matter, she had a bottle in her bedroom. She headed that way.

She pulled the bottle out of her bottom dresser drawer and took a long haul. Instantly she felt better. Her head cleared. She realized her daughter stood in the doorway.

"You're pathetic."

"Katie, please calm down. You don't understand—"

"No, you don't understand, Mom. I don't stay here because of you. I stay because of the kids. But if you're going to keep me prisoner here and embarrass me like that, then I'm going to figure out another way to take care of them."

She put a hand on the top of her dresser to steady herself. "What's that supposed to mean?"

"I don't know yet."

"Are you threatening me?"

"Nope. Not at all. I'm just telling you that starting now, I'm going to try to figure out a new plan. This one isn't working for me anymore. Actually, it never did, but whatever. Now, if you'll excuse me, even though the wind chill is twenty below zero, I'm going to walk to church. Try not to burn the house down while I'm gone."

"Wait."

She stopped. "What?"

Erica searched for words.

"Make it quick, Mom. I don't want to be late."

"You can't walk. It's too far."

"Well, I guess we're going to find out." She started again.

Erica went to the doorway. "Wait. I'll go with you. We'll ... we'll all go."

Katelynn turned around slowly and then laughed. "You can't go anywhere in your condition."

"Give me a second," she said calmly. "Let me get cleaned up. Then I'll have a few drinks, and I'll be able to go. Get your brothers and sisters ready."

Katelynn stared at her for a long time. "You're serious."

"Yes."

"You're not going to turn around, lie down for a rest, and pass out?"

"Pass out? It's ten o'clock in the morning! I'm not that bad!"

Katelynn tipped her head to the side with a look that said, "Oh really?" It might have been the most devastating look she'd ever received.

"I promise. I won't."

"Your promises mean nothing to me." Her words continued to be cruel, but her tone was softening.

"Please, get them ready. I need ten minutes." She swung the door shut and then turned into her room. What a mess. What a mess her whole life was. How had it come to this? She took another long drink, aware of precisely how much alcohol she needed. Enough to get her act together. But not enough to make things worse. She sighed, waiting for the alcohol to kick in. And it did.

She surveyed the mess again. How had it come to this? She knew how. She'd been too sad to move. Too sad to change. Too sad to live. Staying alive only because she had children.

But Katelynn was done. It couldn't continue like this anymore.

Erica had no desire to go to church, but if that's what it would take to keep Katelynn, then she would do it. And besides, maybe they *could* help her. She doubted it, but maybe? She opened her dresser drawer and groaned. What on earth was she going to wear?

She found a long-sleeved striped T-shirt that looked brand-new. She had no idea where it had come from. She paired it with the pants she'd worn yesterday. She brushed and braided her hair and then headed for the bathroom. She brushed her teeth, gargled with mouthwash twice, and put on lipstick and mascara. Then she stepped back and surveyed herself in the mirror.

Huh. That wasn't so bad.

She came out of the bathroom to find her kids waiting in the living room, dressed and bewildered. Katelynn looked surprised to see her. Erica scanned the room for her winter coat and didn't see it anywhere. When was the last time she'd worn it? She'd walked to the gas station a few days ago, hadn't she? She swung her eyes around the room again. So where had she lain her coat when she'd gotten home? Or had she even worn a coat?

She realized Katelynn was holding a coat out toward her. It wasn't hers. "It's probably too small, but maybe it'll work."

She took it. "Is it yours?"

"Yes. From last year. I was saving it for Marcy."

Marcy blinked when she heard her name.

"Thanks, Katie." She had the urge to wrap her arms around her oldest daughter and just hold her, hold her tight forever, but of course she didn't. She slid one arm into the coat and then the other. She wouldn't be able to zip it up, but that was okay. It was on her body. "I'll go see if the car will start. It looks pretty cold out."

"I called Chevon. She can give us a ride."

Erica grimaced but then immediately tried to hide her disgust. She didn't need a teenager driving her around—a pregnant teenager at that.

"She's outside."

Great. Fine. Whatever. She took a deep breath. "Let's go then."

Katelynn held a tin of Altoids out to her.

"I've only had vodka. It shouldn't smell."

"I can smell it." She shoved the tin at her. "Just in case."

Fine. She took the tin and went through her front door. But when she reached the teenager's car, it was almost too much. What was she doing? Going to *church*? Of all the places to go, *that's* what she was doing? And a church in crappy Carver Harbor of all places. Everyone there was going to judge her to death.

"Jason actually let you drive his car?" Katelynn asked.

Oh great. Even better. She was being picked up in the great Jason DeGrave's car.

"I didn't ask permission." She snickered.

Erica stood there with her hand on the door handle. It would be so much easier to go back inside, get warm, and have another drink. Let Katelynn take the kids to church. It wouldn't hurt them any. It would be good for them. She could use an hour of peace and quiet. She started to look back at her house, but Katelynn caught her eye.

"You promised."

She let out a long breath. But Katelynn didn't understand. She didn't know what this was like.

"Fine, Mom. Go back inside. Break your promise, just like always."

She ripped the door open and crawled inside.

"Katelynn," Chevon said, "you could have given your mother shotgun."

"She didn't call it."

Chapter 53

Erica

When Erica saw what church they were going to, she was surprised. This building had been abandoned forever. When she'd heard new church, she'd figured new building. But that was not the case. This was not new. It was ancient. And yet someone had done a lot of touching up. It looked cute. Inviting even. There were new windows, new paint, and a new sign out front.

She studied the sign. New Beginnings Church. That's what she needed, wasn't it? A new beginning. It sounded poetic, but such a thing wasn't even possible. There was no way to wipe the slate clean. Not in real life.

As Chevon stopped the car, church bells rang out, and the beauty of them sent a shiver down Erica's spine. This was weird. She'd heard church bells before and couldn't ever remember being affected by them.

"Does that mean we're late?" Katelynn asked.

"Nah," Chevon said.

A tall woman in a long fur coat and a crazy giant purple hat stood in front of the door. "Does that woman have feathers in her hat?" Erica asked, bewildered.

Chevon snickered. "Yeah, she's nuts. But she's also super nice."

They got out of the car, and panic overcame her. What on earth was she thinking? She looked at Katelynn. "I'm sorry, honey." Her breath was ragged. "I don't think I can."

Katelynn didn't look at her. She was looking at something past her. When Erica turned to follow her gaze, she saw that the woman in the fur coat was approaching. Her panic worsened. She started to open the car door, but Chevon had already locked it.

"Chevon, why don't you take the kids in?" the tall woman said gently.

"Come on." Chevon started walking, and helplessly, Erica watched her kids follow.

Her eyes got hot with tears. She had created a complete nightmare. She was going to have to go inside.

The crazy woman smiled at her and held out a hand. "Hi, I'm Rachel. And you can do this."

Erica looked at that hand, bewildered. What, was she supposed to take it? She wasn't a little kid. She looked up into Rachel's eyes, expecting crazy, expecting belittling, expecting judgment—but she saw nothing but warmth. Who *was* this woman?

"Who are you?" she asked, and then felt foolish for asking.

Rachel laughed quietly. "Just a friend."

Because she didn't know what else to do, she took the offered hand and allowed herself to be led toward the church. When she reached the steps, she heard music, and tears spilled from her eyes. It was beautiful, familiar somehow, even though there was no reason for it to be familiar.

She swallowed hard. She had to get a grip. She was here for her children—not for some delusional redemption effort.

She stepped through the doors, and her eyes were immediately drawn to the high ceilings. But when she brought them back down, she saw Katelynn coming toward her with wide eyes. "Mom, I think Aunt Molly's here."

What? That wasn't possible. Molly didn't even live in Maine anymore, let alone in Carver Harbor. Her eyes scanned the room. "Where?"

"Far left, third row. I don't want to point."

As she looked, the woman in question stood up, and Erica gasped. She was older, her face yellowed with bruises, her hair a different color, but it was Molly. A sob escaped out of Erica. She looked at Katelynn. "What do I do?" Then she looked at Rachel. "What do I do?"

"I should go," Erica said to no one.

"Is Molly your sister?" Rachel asked softly.

Erica nodded. "I haven't seen her in forever, though. She hates me."

"I've talked to Molly about her sister," Rachel said. "And I assure you, she doesn't hate you. Come on, let's go see her." Rachel took her hand again, and Erica realized she hadn't noticed her dropping it in the first place.

She looked at her daughter. "Come with me," she pleaded.

Katelynn, back to her old stalwart, faithful, loving self, nodded.

As Erica crossed the room, conversations stilled, and heads turned to look, as if they somehow knew something significant was about to happen.

Molly didn't see her coming until she was almost there, and then she cried out. The wail sounded as if it came from someone in pain, but the look on her face said otherwise. She came running toward Erica and then flung her arms around her, sobbing over her shoulder.

"What? ... How?" Erica tried to ask.

Molly kept sobbing.

No one was talking now. The music had stopped.

Chapter 54

Chevon

C hevon couldn't believe what she was seeing.

They were *sisters?* What were the chances?

Everyone in the church had stopped talking. Most of them stared. Some of them were obviously trying to be respectful and *not* stare. Even Fiona had stopped playing and was looking on.

Molly let go of Katelynn's mom and stepped back, laughing through her tears. "What are you doing here?"

"What am I doing here? What are you doing here? You live in Massachusetts!"

Molly's face fell. "I haven't lived there in years. We were only there a few months, and Trevor lost his job, so we came back. But you weren't here."

Erica shook her head. "No, I tried to get out, but ..." She looked confused. "It doesn't matter now. I can't believe you're here. What ..." She reached up and touched her cheek. Then she looked down at Molly's cast. "Did Trevor do this?"

Molly gently pushed her hand down. "It doesn't matter now. I'm okay. So you're in Carver Harbor ..." She laughed. "But why are you *in church?*"

She looked at Katelynn. "Katelynn made me come."

Molly's eyes moved to Katelynn's face and then grew wide. "Oh my goodness. Little Katelynn! You're so old!" She stepped away from her sister to wrap her arms around Katelynn, who looked bewildered. She stepped back and looked down at her. "And so beautiful! Remind me how old you are."

Katelynn hesitated. "Sixteen," she whispered.

Chevon felt bad. Katelynn was so embarrassed. Chevon stepped closer to her. This also brought her closer to Jason.

"Are you okay?" he asked.

"Yeah," she said without looking at him. "Why?"

"Because you're crying."

Didn't he know by now that she cried at everything these days? Yesterday she'd cried at a dog food commercial. She wiped her tears away. "I just can't believe it, you know? What are the chances?"

Jason put a hand on the small of her back, and a wonderful warmth spread through her. "Pretty good where God's involved."

She rested her head on his shoulder. Was that what this was? God? God had done this? God had put Roderick Puddy in the right place to save Molly, and God had gotten Katelynn to want to come to church, so that these two sisters could find each other again? Wow.

Wait. An idea occurred to her like a slice of cold air. She had prayed that God would prove himself to her. Was that what this was? Was this God proving himself to her? Had her prayer caused this to happen? She dismissed the thought. No way. She wasn't that big a deal. God wouldn't move a hundred puzzle pieces around just to prove himself to a worm like her.

Would he?

Jason kissed the top of her head. "I can almost feel your mind spinning."

She looked up at him. "I never want to admit you're right, but I think I have some questions."

He let out a long exhale. "I don't think I've ever heard more awesome words. Except for maybe when you said you might marry me."

She giggled. "Yeah, except for that."

Molly took her sister's hand into her good one. Then she turned toward the staring congregation. "Wow, not much privacy in Carver Harbor, is there?"

There was a soft rumble of polite laughter.

Molly took a deep breath. "Not much for public speaking, but since you all have put off starting the church service, I should probably explain why." She said all this still looking at Erica, who looked deathly embarrassed. "This is my long-lost sister, Erica. She's amazing. We used to be best friends. And then life got complicated, and we had a stupid fight, and we lost touch." She turned to the congregation. "I don't know how to thank you all, especially Lauren ... and Vicky ... and Rachel. I didn't want your help, but you gave it to me anyway." She laughed, and others joined her. Vicky's cackle rose above the rest. "But this is definitely the best part of the whole thing. I thought she lived far away. I thought she wouldn't want to see me. But I was wrong. And now I have my sister back." She looked at Lauren. "Thank you." Then she looked at Roderick. "And thank you too. I don't even know your first name, but I should probably tell you that I never liked that window anyway."

A few people laughed.

"Wait," Jason whispered. "What window?"

"Roderick had to break a window to get into her house."

"Oh wow. I always knew that guy was a baller."

Chevon giggled and rolled her eyes. She couldn't believe how good she felt. In this building. With these people. With Jason's arm around her. With God.

Everything was going to be okay.

Chapter 55

Cathy

Cathy couldn't stop crying. She couldn't stop smiling. She couldn't stop praising God. She felt like dancing. Only her New England stoicism prevented her from breaking out into a jig right then and there.

A full fifteen minutes after the service was supposed to start, Pastor invited everyone to sit. Then, as the noise died down, he laughed. "I was hesitant to interrupt all the festivities, but we've got some guests with us today, and they probably have no idea what's going on, so I didn't want them to think that this is how we run a church service." He laughed again. No one joined him. This happened to him a lot. It didn't seem to faze him.

"For those of you who don't know, we spent the month of January trying to reach out into the community, and it seems that God has used this to help these two lovely women find each other again." He nodded toward Erica and Molly. "Praise you, Father." He gripped the pulpit and looked down at it, though Cathy could clearly see there were no notes there to help him. "It was quite a month." He chuckled. "Quite a trip." He looked up. "I think we should do more months like it, but first, God tells us it's important to rest too. Working ourselves to death doesn't help anyone. So let's take a few weeks to recover, refresh, and reflect, shall we? All right, Fiona's going to start doing her thing again here in a minute, and then we'll worship with song. But first, our sister Cathy had something she wanted to share.

Cathy froze. Oh no. She *had* asked him if she could say something—*before* Katelynn's family had walked in. She'd wanted to pray for them, but she wasn't going to do that now. She thought Erica had probably received all the attention she could endure.

Everyone stared at her expectantly. She didn't want to just wave the pastor off. That would make him look foolish.

So she stood. She cleared her throat and smoothed out her skirt. *Give me some words, Father.*

"I just wanted to thank all of you. Pastor was right. January was quite a month, and I thank you all for journeying through it with us. I've so enjoyed getting to know each of you better." She found Chevon's eyes and tried to send her love via a smile.

"I'm so encouraged by all that's been happening here, especially this morning. Isn't it amazing what God can do?"

Several people applauded, and Cathy's heart leapt at the sound.

"I've been reminded these past weeks just how hard life can be. But at the same time, I've been reminded how big God is. He doesn't have to prove himself to us, yet he does it again and again. The older I get, the more evidence I see. The healings, the rescues, the recoveries, the fresh starts. You know, the older I get, the more I believe in new beginnings." She laughed. "And I don't mean the church, though I believe in us too. I mean, *I believe in new beginnings.*"

Acknowledgements

I'm a little scared to write acknowledgements because I might forget someone. Please forgive me! *bites nails*

First, thank you, Faithful Readers. I used to only make up stories in my head. I am so, so grateful I now get to share them with you! Thanks so much for reading.

And thank you to my *amazing* first readers: Julie, Lisa, Susan, Molly, Tammy, and of course, Mom! And thank you to my Splash Team members! You're the best!

And thank you to Faithful Readers: Ann M., for naming the beloved Hissy Fit; and Alice H., for naming Sir Pounciful!

Thank you, husband and children, for putting up with all my writing time. I love you more than words can say. And of course, thank you, Father, for all things.

Books by Robin Merrill

New Beginnings
Knocking
Kicking
Searching
Knitting
Working
Splitting

Shelter Trilogy
Shelter
Daniel
Revival

Piercehaven Trilogy
Piercehaven
Windmills
Trespass

Wing and a Prayer Mysteries
The Whistle Blower
The Showstopper
The Pinch Runner
The Prima Donna

Gertrude, Gumshoe Cozy Mystery Series
Introducing Gertrude, Gumshoe
Gertrude, Gumshoe: Murder at Goodwill
Gertrude, Gumshoe and the VardSale Villain
Gertrude, Gumshoe: Slam Is Murder
Gertrude, Gumshoe: Gunslinger City
Gertrude, Gumshoe and the Clearwater Curse

Made in the USA
Monee, IL
09 May 2023